SUSPICION ON SUGAR CREEK

Susannah B. Lewis

For my mama.

I miss your wit, woman.

ONE

I've often wondered why people bombard the bereaved with gifts of greasy fried chicken, casseroles and pastries. I understand the general premise that providing meals for the brokenhearted is just one less thing for them to worry about in their time of sorrow. I understand that the carbs are actually condolences, a kind gesture of sympathy, but food doesn't deter the mourning from spiraling into deep depression. A cheesy concoction in a Pyrex dish won't fill the void and ease the pain. *I thought my life was over until the pastor's wife brought donuts.* You never hear that.

I stood at my kitchen window and watched a heavyset woman with a round dish containing a pie (or possibly a quiche) bound onto the white porch across the street and ring the doorbell. She shifted from one foot to the other and rang it again. We both peered at the driveway where Baker Kilpatrick's BMW sat covered in rain, and she rang the bell a third time.

She appeared impatient, and she placed the pie (or possibly the quiche) on a red wicker chair next to the front door. Pulling her raincoat tightly around her large body, she walked down the steep porch steps and into the summer drizzle.

"Why won't he come to the door?" I asked my husband, who was sitting on the couch in the living room behind me tapping on his laptop. "Yesterday his porch looked like a buffet. I thought about swiping Mrs. Anderson's spaghetti bake off his steps for supper last night."

"He just lost his wife. He probably didn't want to talk to Mrs. Anderson about her Elvis memorabilia collection for three hours," Tim replied, his eyes never leaving the computer screen.

I looked back out the window as the chunky lady's van disappeared down our sleepy street damp from the summer shower. Then I saw the front door open. Baker Kilpatrick stepped onto the porch, retrieved the pie (or possibly the quiche) and disappeared into the house, the navy blue door slamming behind him.

"He just took the food, Tim! He was home! He took the food!"

I exclaimed from the window saturated with streaks of water.

"So?"

"He didn't want to go to the door!"

"Tessa, the man is grieving. Maybe he doesn't want to talk to anyone. Why don't you get away from the window and find something constructive to do? What happened over there last weekend was tragic, but you've got to let it go. Quit staring at his house."

What happened over there last weekend certainly was tragic. It was like nothing our sleepy little southern community had ever seen, and everyone on our cove, in the coffee shops and diners, and down at the Cut N' Curl was talking about it.

Last Saturday, as I sat on the wrought-iron barstool at my kitchen island, drinking my first cup of morning coffee and reading over the putrid rough draft of my book, I heard the sound of sirens. I left the manuscript covered in red ink next to the sink and darted to the window to see an ambulance pulling up the steep driveway of the French country home across the street.

The girls woke to the blaring sound, and we were glued to the kitchen window for the next thirty minutes. Leigh Kilpatrick was finally wheeled out on a stretcher, a sheet half-covering her lifeless face that was nearly as blue as her front door.

Grace called before the ambulance had taken a right on the Tupelo highway. We met in my front yard, both of us still in our pajamas and bathrobes, and we discussed what we'd seen. As Grace sipped from her mug and patted her short gray curls frizzing in the June humidity, Baker slowly exited his home. He didn't acknowledge us standing there as he casually walked to his BMW and reversed down the driveway.

Baker and Leigh Kilpatrick had been our neighbors for only four months. As they unloaded the U-Haul on that chilly February morning, I walked over to introduce myself and welcome them with a store-bought German chocolate cake that I'd placed in Tupperware and topped with extra pecans to make it look homemade. Within thirty seconds of conversing with them, I'd concluded that Baker Kilpatrick and his wife were both arrogant douchebags. They were very unimpressed with my cake and my conversation. All of their answers to my friendly questions were short and snippy. As I walked back to my house after our short introduction, I was determined never to speak to either of them again. And I was ticked that I'd never see my Tupperware again, too.

Based on our hurried conversation, I'd learned that the Kilpatricks were newlyweds. They were close to my age, late-thirties, and had no children. Baker thought he was attractive; it was evident in his cocky attitude, but his beady eyes, gelled jet-black hair and stout cologne pegged him as a sleaze ball. Leigh was tall, attractive and thin with a blonde pixie cut and pale eyes. She had an icy personality, as he did, but she was certainly too pretty to be hanging on that troll's arm.

Baker was a veterinarian, which I found to be odd since I'd seen him kick the crap out of Grace's cat when it took a dump on his lawn. Leigh was a neonatal nurse, which also surprised me because she seemed like the type to eat babies for brunch. Pleasant people, they definitely were not.

In the few months that they lived on Sugar Creek Cove, they never hosted parties in their elegant home. They were never seen working in their yard or even washing their cars in the driveway. They left for work, came home and then disappeared behind the navy blue door. And that was quite all right by me.

There are only five homes on our sleepy country cul-de-sac. The Andersons live on the corner of Sugar Creek and Highway 78 to Tupelo. They are an older couple who claim to be Elvis' fourth cousins, twice removed, or some such confusing nonsense. They are nice people, but they overkill referencing The King in normal conversation. If I had a nickel for each time they broke into the chorus of "Hound Dog" when my daughter's black and white Lhasa Apso, Oreo, ran into their yard, well, I'd have enough nickels to buy

Graceland (and insist that they move there).

The Parkers live across the street from the Andersons. Mr. Parker is a neurosurgeon and his wife, Nance, studies a rare bacterium that she discovered in fresh water ecosystems (or something brilliant that goes totally over my head every time she tries to explain it to me). They both work long hours being smart and often leave their rambunctious teenage boys home alone. The smell of pot and the sound of gangsta rap wafts down to our house at least three nights a week. I find it completely oxymoronic that three spoiled, rich white boys proudly belt out explicit lyrics about living in the projects. Mrs. Anderson once tried to drown out their melodies with her favorite hard-knock life song– Elvis' "In the Ghetto".

My family, Grace and the Kilpatricks live at the end of the cove. We each have 2-acre lots shaded by magnolia and oak trees, ivy and overgrown hydrangea bushes. Our homes resemble one another with ornamental shutters, arches and accentuating keystones.

Grace McKinney is in her late sixties. We immediately hit it off when Tim and I moved to Sugar Creek Cove nearly ten years ago, but we've spent even more time together since her husband, Jack, died of cancer last summer. Although she is old enough to be my mother, Grace and I have a lot in common. We both love to garden and gossip. We enjoy a quiet game of Rook after church on Sundays and a cup of coffee while trimming the crepe myrtles.

The morning after Leigh Kilpatrick was wheeled out of her home looking like a Smurf, I went for a walk around the cove. Dr. Parker pulled into his driveway as I passed his house, and I gave him a wave.

"Dr. Parker?" I called to him as he exited his Jaguar in wrinkled scrubs.

"Morning, Tessa." He smiled and shuffled towards me while I walked in place in front of his home. "Getting in some cardio?"

"I'm trying. Threw my clean eating out the window last night while watching *The Golden Girls* marathon. I devoured half a cheesecake in one episode, so I figured I ought to go for a walk," I said as Dr. Parker chuckled. "I was wondering if you'd heard about Leigh Kilpatrick."

"Oh, yes," he said as his tired face saddened. "Tragic, isn't it?"

"What happened?" I fished for answers.

"I was on call yesterday morning when they brought her in to North Mississippi Med. She committed suicide."

"No!" I gasped.

"Afraid so." He nodded. "I heard she wrote a note then took a combination of pills and washed them down with a fifth of vodka. I don't know the specifics, and couldn't really divulge if I did, but she was DOA."

"Oh my." I sighed and shook my head. "Grace and I saw the ambulance come and get her, but we had no idea."

"It's such a sad situation. She was a beautiful young woman. I hear she really is, well *was*, one of the best neonatal nurses at the hospital. It's just terrible." He rubbed his drowsy eyes.

"What about her husband? How is he holding up?"

"I'm not sure, Tessa. I don't think I'd even know him if I saw him. I've ever met him before, but Mr. Anderson told me he's probably the one who called the cops on the boys last month. Said they were disturbing the peace with their music, but I've always encouraged them to play classical music loudly. Makes them smart, you know?" He tapped his temple.

I grinned at Dr. Parker and wondered if he knew the effects of Tupac at deafening decibels.

"I've only spoken with him once, and he wasn't a very nice guy. He's kind of arrogant and moody. Still, though, I hate to hear this news about his wife," I said.

"Sure is a shame." He stifled a yawn.

"You're tired, Dr. Parker. I'll let you get inside and rest."

"Have a good one, Tessa." The doctor waved at me and headed for his home, stepping over a half-smoked joint in his driveway. For such an intelligent fella, he was dumb as a doornail when it came to his boys' shenanigans.

I glanced down at the Kilpatrick residence, ivy growing along the north side of the house, and chills ran down my spine. Leigh Kilpatrick was dead, and despite my original feelings about her husband, I couldn't help but to feel sad for the poor guy…and curious about the entire situation.

I hadn't taken my eyes off his house since.

TWO

I spend Tuesdays with Rusty Ballard. I am not fond of Tuesdays with Rusty Ballard. Every Tuesday morning, for eleven weeks now, I roll out of bed and shuffle to my coffee maker, sighing and groaning the entire length of the hallway because I will soon see Rusty Ballard.

Rusty Ballard sent me an email in March with the subject line, "I NEED YOU." I assumed that it was some kind of porn spam message, so I filed it in my junk folder without even reading it. A few days later, though, Rusty called my home. When I answered the phone, he said the same thing, "I need you… to help me write a book."

When I graduated from Mississippi State sixteen years ago, I went to work for Tupelo's *Daily Journal.* I quit the journalism gig to be a stay-at-home mother before my first daughter was born. Somewhere along the line, though, I became a freelance writer. Now I regularly contribute parenting pieces to my editor in New York, Gabriella.

I crank out ten articles for Gab each month, and she sells them to magazines and websites across the country. With the payment from the articles, I can afford to pitch in on the electricity bill. Although not a lucrative business, freelance writing has given me a lot of exposure which I hope will be beneficial when I finally finish the stupid book I've been working on for the last five years.

Rusty is a Tupelo boy who found me through one of my articles published on Yahoo!, and since I was local, he thought I'd be the perfect candidate to help him write his book. I don't know why I told Rusty Ballard that I'd work with him, but, alas, I did. So now I spend every Tuesday helping Rusty write a manuscript about a chain-smoking cyclist who hopes to win a gold medal and the girl of his dreams.

"Cody has to help Mary move into her new apartment," Rusty screeched when I opened the door and he marched inside.

"Good morning, Rusty." I yawned and shuffled behind him as

he sat at the farm table in my kitchen.

Rusty was a tall, thin, hippie guy with a patchy beard, messy hair and Lennon-esque transition glasses that often malfunctioned. I once turned on the ceiling light and he suddenly looked like Roy Orbison sitting before me. He said the illumination of his dashboard caused his spectacles to change into sunglasses, too– even at night. I often sang the 80's Corey Hart tune about wearing sunglasses at night to Rusty, which annoyed him to no end.

"Cody loves Mary. He will do anything to win her love. Of course he would help her move!" Rusty pulled the thick manuscript from his torn messenger bag and placed it on the table.

"Rusty, the man is a chain-smoker. He coughs more than he speaks throughout the entire novel. How is he going to help her move her sofa up seven flights of stairs?" I sat at the table and thumbed through what he'd written so far.

"He has his inhaler," Rusty argued.

"Can't she at least move to an apartment on the ground floor? I mean, come on, Rusty! Seven flights of stairs!"

"She has to live on the seventh floor. She has to have an apartment overlooking the bike path at the park. She has to be able to see him biking every day. It has to be that way!"

"Look, I know we've discussed this before, but I'm still confused. How is Cody going to successfully compete in the marathon? I mean, he's not in the best health. He'll be coughing up a lung with every pedal. Is Cody going to die on race day?"

"No! We can't kill Cody. I've already told you the ending that I've envisioned. He rides into the sunset with Mary sitting on his handlebars. That's the ending!"

Rusty's story was asinine. He always shot down my recommendations to spruce it up a bit. He'd had this story in his head for years and wasn't open to my suggestions. Rusty only wanted me to edit grammatical errors. He didn't know the difference between a semicolon and a colon, so I advised him with that kind of thing. I helped him correct sentences like, *Cody coughed; then he lit another Camel and mounted his Schwinn.*

"Okay, Rusty. He will help Mary move. She will live on the seventh floor. He will stop and smoke at every water station." I stood and walked to the coffee pot. "Do you want some?"

"No." He quickly shook his head and pulled his laptop from his bag. "What about the new character I mentioned last week? Artie? Do you think he's a good fit for the story?"

Rusty had a dream (marijuana-induced, no doubt) a few weeks ago about a beatnik named Artie who sold sausages on the corner of Haight and Ashbury. Now he was a hot dog vender at the marathon with sage advice for Cody, the smoking and lovesick cyclist.

"What kind of advice is Artie going to give Cody? Is he going to tell him to quit smoking? Is he going to tell him that moving Mary's chest of drawers up seven flights of stairs may send the guy to an early grave? I can tell you that. We don't need Artie."

"Sometimes I wonder if you believe in this story, Tessa." Rusty pouted.

Rusty Ballard is an unemployed 22-year-old sarcastic kid who still lives at home with his parents, and the only goal in his life is to finish this book about the smoking cyclist. *Ten Speeds of Love* is his life's passion no matter how stupid I deem it to be, so I often feel guilty for not believing in it.

As a fellow writer, I sympathize with Rusty. I sympathize with having a story stuck in your head and the incessant need to get it out. That's the only reason I continue to allow him in my home on Tuesday mornings. Besides, the kid is paying me $20 bucks every week to place commas where they are needed. Between that and my freelance money, Tim will be able to retire early.

"I believe in your story, Rusty," I lied and sat back at the table with the cup of black brew in my hand. "If you think Artie is pivotal to the plot then, by all means, add him. You and Artie and Mary's seventh story apartment have my blessing."

Rusty opened his laptop and began typing furiously as wrinkles gathered on his brow. He always chewed on his bottom lip and regularly pushed the transition glasses up his nose when he was in the zone like this. I knew it was best to keep quiet while he focused on the dialogue between Artie, the hot dog vendor, and the cyclist with impending emphysema.

As he typed, I twirled my long pony tail around my fingers, gazed out the kitchen window and caught a glimpse of Baker Kilpatrick's white BMW pulling up his driveway. I quickly stood as the kitchen chair scraped across the cherry hardwood floor, and I dashed over to the window to investigate.

Baker exited his car with shopping bags in both hands and a bottle of liquor tucked under his armpit. He shut the car door with his foot and jovially walked to his garage. I swore he was smiling.

"Well, look at that," I mumbled to myself, wondering why a man who was supposed to be bereaved appeared so happy-go-lucky. "Strange."

"You're breaking my concentration, Tessa," Rusty groaned from his keyboard.

I mumbled an apology as Baker disappeared into his home.

"What is it?" Rusty sighed as if my quiet grumbling had ruined his writing session and his life. "What are you mumbling about?"

"The guy across the street. His wife just died and he looks like he's about to throw a party." I went back to the kitchen table. "He was smiling."

"Baker Kilpatrick?" Rusty asked.

"You know him?" I sat down.

"My oldest brother dated Leigh for a while. He went to her funeral last week."

"You didn't tell me that last Tuesday!" I slapped at his scrawny, hairy arm poking out of a tattered Widespread Panic t-shirt. "Why didn't you tell me that? You knew she lived across the street and you never told me she dated your brother?"

"I'm telling you now," he said, shrugging.

"Well? Does your brother know why she killed herself?" I attentively leaned into Rusty and pressed the mug to my lips.

"She and my brother, Ralphie, lived together for a while. She left him for Baker about two years ago."

"You have a brother named Ralphie? Rusty and Ralphie?" I

grinned.

"Yeah, so?" He smirked. "I've got two other brothers named Ricky and Randy. What's the problem?"

"Nothing, Rusty." I shook my head and swallowed my giggle. "It's cute. I'm all for alliterative sibling names."

"Yeah, anyway." Rusty rolled his eyes behind the glasses that were tinting as the sun shone through the bay window. "She had a drug problem. She went into treatment twice while she dated my brother. Then she left Ralphie for Baker Kilpatrick. Ralphie said it was because he was a vet and had access to horse tranquilizers."

"Are you kidding?" My eyes grew wide. "She was on horse tranqs?"

"Of course she wasn't!" He chuckled at my naiveté. "She worked in a hospital, Tessa! She had access to all the drugs she could get! Ralphie made up the horse tranquilizer thing out of anger and jealousy. He wanted everyone to believe that a woman would have to be really desperate to leave him. He hates to admit that Baker Kilpatrick is simply more handsome and more successful than Ralphie Ballard, the avid comic book collector and Rainbow vacuum salesman."

"But she really was on drugs? You think that's why she killed herself?" I wondered.

Rusty said, "Leigh was smoking hot, but she was a crazy one. I was there when she threatened to set Ralphie on fire one night because he ordered pineapple on her pizza. She's been out of her mind since she did LSD at Lollapalooza 97."

"I knew she was rude, but I didn't know she was a drug addict. To think I took her a German chocolate cake from Piggly Wiggly when she'd rather I sent over acid."

"Baker has his own problems, too." Rusty looked back to his computer.

"What's wrong with Baker, aside from being a jerk? Is he on horse tranquilizers?"

"No one was on horse tranquilizers, Tessa. Ralphie made that up."

"What's wrong with Baker?" I repeated.

"Ralphie said he's been married a couple of times and was arrested for beating on his old ladies. A real Ike Turner, that one."

"I knew it!" I banged my fist on the cream farm table. "The first time I spoke to him, I knew he was the type to do that sort of thing. I saw him kick Grace's cat once. You'd think veterinarians would be kind people. Animal lovers, you know?"

"He's no people lover, that's for sure. The dude's got a record. Ralphie told Leigh all the bad things he'd heard about Baker, but she didn't care. I love my brother, but it's sad that a woman would choose an abusive veterinarian over him. If he'd just quit droning on about Thor and Rainbow vacuums. He's 35-years-old and wore a winged helmet and threw dirt all over Grandma's floor last Christmas just so he could demonstrate a new model."

"That must be why she killed herself. He was pounding on her all of the time. That's why they never had parties or people over. That's why she did it." I convinced myself. "Thank you, Rusty. You just added a substantial piece to that puzzle."

"Can we get back to *my* puzzle here, Tessa?" He nodded at his computer.

That was the first Tuesday I was glad to have Rusty Ballard sitting at my kitchen table. I was glad to have him there because we were finally talking about a real story instead of an asthmatic love-sick cyclist.

THREE

When I wrenched my back playing powder-puff football for an elementary school fundraiser a few years ago, Dr. Pulaski prescribed me pain killers. The Percocet helped my back, but they certainly didn't help my bowels. I've never experienced such tormenting and relentless constipation in all my life. It was like I'd eaten fourteen loaves of bread and a block of cheese. I just sat there, stopped up for hours upon hours, and that blockage finally morphed me into a wretched beast that sent children and small animals scurrying for cover. Writer's block is *exactly* the same.

Five years of my thirties have been wasted writing and erasing and re-writing a stupid story about a woman who finds love and a murder charge on the French Riviera. Five years of tormenting bouts of writer's block. Five years of mind constipation.

I know the writer's block stems solely from the fact that I've never been to the French Riviera. I've begged Tim to take me for creative stimulation, but we just can't afford to make the trip. I've read thousands of *Conde Nast Traveler* magazines and scoured the internet for inspiration about the far-off place, but it isn't the same as actually going.

My oldest daughter, Jules, often tells me that I should just change the setting to some place I've been before like Fairfax, Indiana or Gulf Shores, Alabama. But in my mind, the story of Penelope Broussard takes place on the French Riviera. I can't picture another setting. I just cannot picture this woman living in the United States, eating corn dogs and driving a Celica.

Much like Rusty Ballard's obsession with telling the story of a cyclist with COPD, completing the stupid script about a French woman has become my fixation. And I'll never complete the stupid script because of the writer's block. And I'll never get rid of the writer's block until I visit the French Riviera.

Every morning, once Tim has left for the realtor office and my coffee is piping hot, I sit on the wrought-iron barstool at our kitchen island. I pull a green binder from the catch-all drawer and stare at the manuscript.

I've handwritten all 57,482 putrid words of it because I prefer to write by hand instead of to type. I've marked through nearly every single rotten word with a red Bic pen. I want so badly to finish it, to actually type it into a computer document and email it to Gabriella in New York, who promises to pitch it to all of her publishing buddies, but I can't. You know, because of the writer's block. The mind constipation.

After I've stared at the handwritten pages for three hours, dark Folgers and rage soaring through my veins, I finally sigh in disgust and throw it back into the drawer, vowing to forget the story and burn it in the patio fire pit. Then I turn on my laptop and work on my articles.

Writing articles comes easy to me. I have no trouble doting out advice for parents raising teenagers who hate the world and everyone in it. 5000 words on the stress of being a PTO mom effortlessly flow from my fingers. Those are things I know, but that harlot Penelope with her mysterious lover from Monaco just won't tell me her stupid story because I've never been to the French Riviera.

"Still constipated?" Jules shuffled into the kitchen with Oreo at her heels. Sleep boogers had settled in the corner of her caramel eyes, her almond-colored hair was in a messy ponytail atop her head and the long white t-shirt gleamed against her tanned skin.

"You know I am. Dang that French Riviera," I said, finishing off my fifth cup of caffeine.

"I'm telling you, Mother, you've got to change the setting. You can't write in detail about a place if you've never been there. It's impossible." She opened the refrigerator and searched for the milk.

"I once wrote a little ditty that took place in the northwest, and I've never been there. It was really good. It won that short story contest, remember?"

"That was a fictional place. You invented that town in Washington after watching *Twilight* with me. All you had to envision were forests and Redwoods and gray skies. You didn't have to worry about accents and real landmarks and what side of the road the cars drive on and currency exchange." She filled a glass and rolled her eyes. "Duh."

"I'm not in the mood for this, Jules. Don't wake up at noon and start ragging my setting again," I said, slamming the "World's Greatest Mother" mug down on the granite counter.

"It's summer vacation. What do you care how late I sleep in?"

"Jules, just what *are* you doing up in your room all night that makes you sleep until noon every day?"

"I'm certainly not up there writing novels about the French Riviera. I've never been there." She winked at me sassily and left the kitchen, Oreo following closely behind.

Sometimes it's hard to believe that Jules, my first born, used to be a mama's girl. She was my best friend, my helper, my sidekick. She really thought I hung the moon. She took my word solely because it was mine. Five years ago, when she was only nine, my fresh new story about the mysterious French girl excited her. She was sure that it would be a best seller. She was so proud of her mama, the writer.

But then my sweet little Jules turned fourteen. She suddenly needed a training bra and deodorant. She discovered my old Nirvana CD's and boys decked head-to-toe in Under Armour. Her friends were all glued to smartphones and hated their mothers, too. And everything I said was suddenly the stupidest thing that any lame 38-year-old mother has ever muttered in the history of lame 38-year-old mothers.

"Good morning, Mama." Sweet Ellis interrupted my thoughts of a once-sweet Jules.

"Little girl," I said and smiled lovingly at her, "it hasn't been morning for hours. Are you just waking up, too?"

"Yes, ma'am," she replied. Ma'am. The child still addressed me with ma'am.

"Why did *you* stay up so late?" I asked as she searched the pantry for Pop-Tarts, her long wavy hair hanging in her blue eyes.

"I was watching old home movies. I fell asleep in the middle of Christmas 2008. That was the year Santa brought that stuffed My

Little Pony. Rainbow Dash. Remember?"

"Be still my heart," I said under my breath and smiled at her. Jules wouldn't watch a home movie if I paid her in free eye-roll passes.

"How's the book coming along this morning, uh, afternoon?" she asked kindly as she popped the pastries into the toaster.

"It's not coming along, Ellis. It never is," I grumbled and stood from the stool.

"I'm sure it's going to be great, Mama." She grinned at me with her toothy 10-year-old smile that would soon require braces.

I pulled her to my chest and kissed the top of her blonde, soft, strawberry-scented head. "Don't turn into a sarcastic teenager, Ellis. Promise me you'll stay as sweet as you are this morning."

She nodded, grabbed her piping-hot tarts and left me alone in the kitchen. I rinsed the stained coffee cup in the sink and peered out the window to the street. There was Baker Kilpatrick washing his wife's red Mustang in his driveway. He was scrubbing the soft top convertible with white bubbles. He was whistling. The man was whistling.

As I gawked at him through the rolled-open kitchen window above my sink, the phone rang.

"Hello?" I reached for it on the counter without breaking my stare.

"Baker Kilpatrick is washing his wife's car, Tessa. I've never seen that man outside in my life, with the exception of kicking innocent felines or grabbing a plate of chicken off his porch. He's outside, in the daylight. I was so sure he was a vampire," Grace grumbled into the phone.

"I see him, Grace. He's whistling. His lips are pursed. He's either whistling or doing the duck face. Forty-year-old men don't do the duck face. He must be whistling." I continued to stare as he reached for the hose and rinsed the shiny sports car.

"He's happy. His wife has only been in the ground a week, and he's *happy*." I could picture Grace shaking her head as she spoke.

"I think so, too. I saw him walk in yesterday with a bottle of liquor. It's like he's—"

I quit speaking when he opened the soaking car door and taped a for sale sign inside the back window.

"He's already selling her car?" I gasped.

"He's celebrating, that's exactly what he's doing! He's glad she's gone!"

"Grace, you don't think? You don't think he had something to do with her death, do you? Dr. Parker said she took pills."

"I don't know, but I wasn't outside washing Jack's pick-up and doing the duck face days after he died," she declared. "I wanted to hold onto Jack's things as long as I could, not sell them. I do believe this Baker Kilpatrick fellow is a bastard."

"Maybe he's a murdering bastard?" I suggested.

"Maybe," she said. I silently nodded in agreement.

That evening, I watched my handsome husband pull the baby blue tie from his shirt collar and hang it in his closet. "So the man was washing his car? What's the big deal?"

"He was washing his *dead wife's* car," I corrected him as I sat on the bed and covered my dry hands in honeysuckle-scented lotion, "and then he put a for sale sign in it! He's already getting rid of her things, Tim!"

"Well, she can't wash it or drive it, can she?" He disappeared into the bathroom.

"It's so odd, though. We've never seen this man outside before, and we've certainly never seen him whistling or carrying liquor into the house. It's like Grace said, he's celebrating. His wife just died and he's celebrating! He's selling her belongings and celebrating!" I scoffed and pulled back the paisley comforter on our plush bed.

"Tessa." He exited the bathroom in his white t-shirt and boxer shorts. "Washing and selling a car is not a form of celebration. Everyone grieves differently. I think you and Grace are reading too much into this. Leave the poor guy alone."

"Rusty's brother dated Leigh. She was on horse tranquilizers, Tim! She was on drugs, *and* Baker beat her. What if he put a gun to her head and told her to take those pills, huh? We could have a murderer living across the street. Doesn't that concern you?" I pulled the ponytail holder from my long blonde hair and slipped into the bed.

"Your overactive imagination concerns me. You watch too much *Alfred Hitchcock Presents*. Remember when that unmarked van was at Mr. and Mrs. Anderson's all afternoon? You were absolutely convinced someone had murdered them in their home, but they were having their guest room painted?" He crawled beside me and switched off the lamp on his bedside table.

"You said you wouldn't bring that up again! And I don't have an overactive imagination. I have writer's block," I scoffed and threw my head onto the pillow.

"Tessa, please don't blame your mind constipation on me again. I can't—"

"Maybe he killed her because she wouldn't take him to the French Riviera," I huffed and turned away from him.

"Tessa, sweetheart," he said as he reached for me in the dark, "I know you're frustrated. You know I would take you to the Riviera if I could. The shoddy housing market is hurting us all. People are too broke to buy real estate from me, which means we are too poor to take a trip to France. I really wish we could, but we can't. We've already dipped into Jules' college fund and Ellis will need braces soon. She's got a molar coming in sideways. We just can't go right now."

I sighed. "I know. I'm sorry."

"Maybe you should start a new book. Maybe one about a neighbor who murdered his wife with horse tranquilizers?" He leaned over and kissed the top of my head.

"Maybe so," I thought aloud. "I wouldn't have to travel anywhere for inspiration."

FOUR

My mother only calls me two or three times a year, and she only calls when I'm busy. It's like she telepathically knows, "Tessa is occupied. Phone her now." Her name never flashes across the caller ID while I'm watching *The Golden Girls* reruns or having a quiet cup of coffee on the patio.

But she was sure to dial my number while I was enjoying a rare breakthrough and scribbling an entire chapter about Penelope Broussard frolicking on a French coastline that I couldn't accurately envision. She called at the very moment Jules was storming down the court, on the verge of making the winning layup. She wanted to chat while Tim and I had that loving look in our eyes like we did when we were newlyweds. She needed to speak to me when I was walking into the school, the church or the grocery store.

My mother and I have never been close. My father was killed in a car accident when I was only three and my mom, who was a well-respected mortgage lender at a big bank in downtown Jackson, Mississippi, lost her marbles. She quit her productive job and sent my older sister Darcy and me to live with our dad's parents in Starkville. Every day, our unemployed mother sat in our home in Jackson eating Duncan Hines frosting out of a can and chain-smoking Winstons.

When she finally pulled her fat backside out of her recliner in the 80's, she took a job tending bar at some biker joint. Every year she brought a different leather-clad gentleman with a mullet to Christmas dinner at our grandparents' house in Starkville (when she actually came to Christmas dinner).

Although my mother was a wreck, I lived a normal and happy childhood with my grandparents. I was introduced to Tim at Mississippi State, and our wedding was the first time he met my mother. She bounded down to the front pew at First Baptist Church with a scruffy guy named Dirk on her arm. She was wearing an ill-fitting sundress that showed more breast than a Kentucky Fried Chicken commercial. Nanny and Papa asked her to cover her tattooed boobs (or at least put on Dirk's biker jacket with the words

"Mississippi Misfits" stitched across the back), but their suggestion ticked her off. She cussed them (and an innocent wedding planner) and left before I walked down the aisle.

I didn't see her again until my grandmother's funeral several years later. Jules was just a baby and screamed her head off when my mother tried to hold her. I guess babies don't like the stench of nicotine and White Rain hairspray.

My mom has only seen her grandchildren a couple of times, but we do just fine without her. Still, she never ceases to call when I'm busy.

"Tessa, are you busy?" She exhaled smoke into the receiver as I walked into Piggly Wiggly.

Of course I am, I thought.

"Ellis and I are doing some grocery shopping. What's up?"

"I want to take a trip to Atlanta to visit the family cemetery. I need you to drive me."

Oh, did I fail to mention that my mother only calls when I'm busy *and* when she needs something?

"My friend was going to take me, but I can't ride on his bike that far. My back is a wreck. I need you to drive me," she complained.

"I'm not going to be able to drive you to Georgia. I've got a lot going on right now." I threw my heavy purse into the shopping cart.

"Is it Karen?" Ellis mouthed as I nodded. She rolled her eyes, just like her sister does, but it was okay considering the circumstances.

"Come on, Tessa. I really need you to do this for me," her deep smoker's voice bellowed.

"Could you at least ask how I'm doing, how Tim and the girls are doing, before you ask me for favors?" I motioned for Ellis to toss a bag of apples into the buggy.

"How are you and Tim and the kids, Tessa?" she snapped.

"We're fine. Thanks for asking."

"Good. I need a ride to Georgia."

"I just can't do it."

"What about your sister? Is she too busy to take her old mother to Georgia to put flowers on her parents' graves? She won't answer my calls. Maybe you could ask her?" she whined.

"Mom, Darcy is swamped with three boys and her catering business. It's summertime. It's wedding season. I doubt she'll have time to chauffer you to Atlanta. Can't one of your gentlemen friends put you in a sidecar or something?"

"Okay, Tessa. Thanks for nothing." The call ended as I sighed in disgust and tossed my phone into my purse.

"Don't let her get to you, Mama."

"Thanks honey. Every time she calls, I just–" I stopped midsentence when I saw Baker Kilpatrick enter the store. "Let's just forget Karen and finish our shopping, okay?"

I hadn't seen Baker since he was washing his dead wife's Mustang and duck-face whistling all over the driveway a few days before. But there he was now, in Piggly Wiggly, dumping three boxes of modified corn puff cereal into his shopping cart.

"Why don't you buy this good syrup any more, Mama?" Ellis examined the tall plastic bottle.

"It's full of toxins," I answered and motioned for her to put it back on the shelf, and then reached for the organic maple in a glass jar. "High-fructose corn syrup and other crap you can't even pronounce. You don't want that in your body."

"So what's in the fancy maple syrup you buy?"

"Maple syrup, that's what's in it." I watched Baker arrogantly strut to the next aisle. "Come on."

"So you pay five more dollars for maple syrup that only has maple syrup in it?" She shook her head, confused.

I turned onto the next aisle but kept my distance from Baker. "Why isn't he at work?" I mumbled to myself.

"Who are you talking about?"

"The neighbor."

"The vet?" Ellis asked as he mulled over the choices of boxed noodles and powdered sauce.

I eyed his Ole Miss T-shirt and khaki shorts. "He's not even wearing work clothes. It's Wednesday afternoon. Don't dogs and cats get sick on Wednesdays?"

"Maybe he's still too upset about his wife to go back to work. Why do you care?" She reached for tortillas.

"I don't care," I said. "Get the whole wheat ones."

"Mama, they taste like dust. Can't we get the white ones?"

"No. We do whole wheat now."

"Healthy eating is terrible," she mumbled.

"You sound like your sister, Ellis. You promised you wouldn't turn into your angry teenage sister just yet," I said. "He's moving. Let's go."

"Why are we following the dog doctor?" She grudgingly tossed the brown tortillas into the basket.

"We aren't following him. I'm just concerned about him since his wife died."

"Pop-Tarts! I didn't get Pop-Tarts!" Ellis remembered her favorite food.

"Go get the Tasty Pastries instead. They're organic."

"Mama, don't take my Pop-Tarts!" She clung dramatically onto my pink tank top with desperation in her eyes. "Please, I'm begging you. I'll eat spinach and dusty tacos, but don't take my Pop-Tarts. Please! For the love, Mother. Please."

"One box, that's it. You aren't going to sit around eating those artificially-dyed Pop-Tarts all summer. We're getting the Tasty Pastries next time."

"Okay." She darted away as I followed Baker Kilpatrick to the next aisle.

I quietly watched him browse the deodorant. I grimaced when I thought about him pounding on his poor drug-addicted wife and probably forcing her to take a handful of pills. As I imagined terrible scenarios, his eyes left an oversized Degree display and caught mine. I quickly diverted the eye contact by looking down and reaching for whatever was on the shelf in front of me.

"Vanessa?" his raspy voice called.

"Tessa," I corrected him and nervously tucked my hair behind my ear. "How are you, Baker?"

He said nothing and pushed his shopping cart of junk food toward me.

"I've um, I've been thinking about you. I was so sorry to hear about Leigh." I tried to avoid looking into his murky green eyes.

"Well, we've all got to go sometime," he said casually. I made a conscious effort not to let my jaw drop and hit my flip flops. "She always did the grocery shopping. This is the first time I've even been in here."

"I've, uh, been meaning to come over and bring you a meal or something." I awkwardly shifted my weight from one foot to the other.

"If you're one of those health nuts, you can keep your meal." He motioned at my cart of organic food.

"Oh," I said and swallowed, "I, um, I'm not a *health nut*, but I try to make, um, good choices, you know?"

"I don't see the point. We're all going to die of something. Might as well eat the good stuff." He held up a box of Cookie Crisp.

"Yeah, I guess."

"Looks like eating healthy hasn't helped with your problem, though, has it?" He pointed to the large plastic package in my hands. "Isn't there a grain or fruit or something for that?"

"What?" I asked.

"Incontinence?" he smirked as I looked down to the pack of adult diapers I was holding. My face turned a shade of crimson.

"Oh? These?" I chuckled. "No, these are for, um, for my grandmother," I lied and immediately envisioned Nanny cursing me from the grave. She lived to be 87 and never once peed herself.

"Yeah, right." He grinned. "Good luck with your bird food, Vanessa, *and your leakage*. See you around."

I stood on aisle 8 of Piggly Wiggly with adult diapers in my arms and shock covering my face because Baker Kilpatrick had the gall to criticize my food choices and my alleged uncontrollable urination. The scent of his stout cologne and the vision of his mean, beady eyes remained, and I was more convinced than ever that if he hadn't killed his wife, then his malice had driven her to suicide.

FIVE

On Tuesday morning, warm June rain streamed down the oversized kitchen window. Sitting at the farm table in a Dark Side of the Moon t-shirt and holey khaki pants, Rusty tapped his hairy fingers on the keyboard.

"You need a comma to separate two complete clauses," I said while peering at his computer screen.

"Thanks." He backspaced and inserted the comma.

"What advice is Artie giving Cody in this chapter? Still hasn't suggested smoking cessation has he?"

"Cody is a smoker, Tessa. Deal with it," Rusty snapped.

"I know, I know." I leaned back in the kitchen chair and yawned. "So…what else can you tell me about this Baker fellow? I ran into him at the grocery store last week. I'm wondering—"

"I don't want to talk about Baker Kilpatrick. I'm in the zone." He pushed the round glasses up his nose.

"In the zone." I clicked my tongue. "Sorry."

I sat quietly and picked at my nails while Rusty furiously typed. Then I reached for Ellis' latest *Goosebumps* read in the chair next to me and flipped through it, bored with Rusty's writing session.

"What's another word for cough?" He rubbed his hands through his dark shaggy hair. "Hack? Can we use hack?"

"What about 'cleared mucus from his lungs'? Is that too lengthy?" I continued thumbing through the old R.L. Stein paperback.

"Ugh," Rusty groaned and tossed his glasses to the table. He rubbed his eyes in frustration. "I hate to admit you're right, but there are only so many words for cough!"

"You are correct, sir. I am right."

"I need a break," he said and exhaled slowly. "I don't even drink coffee, but I need some caffeine."

I pointed at the half-empty pot on the kitchen counter behind us as Rusty stood from the table. "Mugs are in the cabinet on the left."

He filled a pink polka dot cup and sat back at the table with me. We both sipped the Folgers and watched the rain fall onto the massive magnolia in the front yard as thunder rumbled in the distance.

"Since you're out of the zone, can we talk about Baker Kilpatrick now?" I gripped the warm mug in both of my hands.

"Why are you so curious about the Kilpatricks?"

"Forgive me, Rusty, if my neighbor's suicide conjures up a little curiosity," I said as he put his glasses back on. "What do you know about Leigh? Does she have family around here or anything?"

"Leigh's parents live in Florida, I think. I'm not sure if they even went to the funeral. I know they were estranged because of Leigh's drug use. She was on bad terms with her sister, too." He slurped from the cup.

"She's got a sister? Had a sister?" I asked.

"Yeah, she had a twin. Laurel. I don't think she and Leigh have spoken in years. I don't think she was at the funeral, either. I remember Leigh saying at one time that she was out west somewhere, and she was on drugs also. Laurel may not even know her sister is dead, and if she does, she probably doesn't care." Rusty shrugged.

"That's terrible," I replied and peered at the dreary house across the street, rain rushing down the roof. "The poor girl had family dysfunction, drug problems, addicted to horse—"

"I should've never brought up horse tranquilizers."

"Not to mention she was married to a real douchebag," I sneered. "After my encounter with him at Piggly Wiggly a few days ago, I can see why she was miserable and wanted a way out."

"Wow, you had an encounter with Baker Kilpatrick down at the Piggly Wiggly, huh? Do tell," Rusty said sarcastically as he rested his elbows on the table.

"He made fun of my organic food and my incontinence." I angrily slammed my cup to the placemat.

"You're incontinent?" Rusty cocked his head.

"I'm not, but he assumed I was because I was holding a package of adult diapers."

"Why were you holding adult diapers?"

"I was tailing him in the store and picked them up as a diversion. Even if I was incontinent, wouldn't that be a terrible thing to make fun of? What kind of heartless bastard laughs about incontinence?"

"The same kind of bastard who beats his old ladies, I guess." Rusty shrugged.

"I just can't help but think he had something to do with her death. Is that crazy? I mean, it's not crazy, is it?" I searched Rusty's scruffy face for agreement.

"I think Baker is a real tool, Tessa, but is he a murderer? I doubt it." He shook his head.

"But he's celebrating, Rusty. He's drinking liquor and gouging on Hamburger Helper and washing and selling cars and smiling and whistling. Is that acceptable behavior if your spouse has just died?" I grabbed my cup and stood to refill it.

"Maybe that's his way of dealing with it. Or maybe he is glad she killed herself." He turned in the kitchen chair to face me as I picked up the coffee pot. "It's kind of like an old dog I once had. I loved that dog for years. I'd never hurt that dog, but when it died, I was kind of relieved I didn't have to clean up his crap anymore, you know? Maybe it's a relief that Leigh is gone. Maybe he doesn't have to worry about cleaning up her crap anymore. He doesn't have to worry about her being on drugs anymore. Maybe he's sad about it and grieving, but it's probably also a relief, you know? Is that so wrong? Is it wrong to celebrate a new beginning without her?"

I shrugged, sighed and walked back to the table as Jules entered the kitchen, her faithful Oreo at her bare heels.

"Hey, Rusty," she said as she rummaged through the refrigerator.

"Hey, Jules." He glanced over at her and then focused on the laptop setting before him.

"Seriously? Kale and grapes? That's all we have to eat?" she complained.

"And grilled chicken, salad, apples, hummus and celery. That all sounds like acceptable sustenance to me, Jules," I replied.

She rolled her eyes and popped a grape into her mouth before joining us at the kitchen table. "How's the writing this morning,

Rusty?"

"Oh," he heaved a sigh," I'm kind of stuck right now. Your mother and I can't think of another word for cough."

I quietly exhaled, took another swig and stared out the window.

"Hack?" she suggested.

"You think hack is okay?" He looked over at her as she nodded.

"*You think hack is okay?*" I repeated.

"Sure. I think hack would be fine," she repeated.

"Jules, why don't you tell him to slap a nicotine patch on Cody in the first chapter and we won't have to worry about synonyms for cough?" I suggested.

"He's a smoker, woman! That's part of the story. When I picture Cody Martin, I picture him smoking a Camel. I always have! That's part of him. He smokes! Doesn't your main character have something about her? Some specific trait or habit or hobby? What is it?" He and Jules both gawked at me.

"Well," I said and thought for a moment, "she's allergic to shellfish. I guess—"

"There you go. Penelope Broussard is allergic to shellfish. That's how you created her. Now picture her eating shrimp. Can you picture Penelope eating shrimp?!" he exclaimed.

"No." I shook my head. "I guess I can't."

"My point exactly!" He wildly waved his arms in the air.

"Geez, Rusty. Chill. I'll brew you some decaf next time."

"I think it's great that he has a thing like that, Rusty. It makes Cody who he is. I think a chain-smoking athlete is a wonderful character." Jules scooped Oreo into her lap and rubbed his chocolate ears. "It sounds like a really good story."

"Well, thank you, Jules." Rusty shot angry eyes toward me as I sighed in exasperation.

My daughter— my lovely first born— had nothing but negative things to say about Penelope Broussard frolicking up and down beaches that I've never seen. She thought it was asinine that Penelope fell in love with a Monegasque thug who implicated her in murder, but she thought the story of Cody, the overemotional cyclist who hot-boxed more cancer sticks than my own mother, was a best-seller. In that moment, I was annoyed... and jealous.

"Well, good luck." She stood from the table with her furry friend in her arms. "I can't wait to read it when it's done."

"I appreciate the support," Rusty said as Jules disappeared from the kitchen.

I rolled my eyes at the cohorts and looked out the kitchen window to see that the pounding rain had abruptly become merely a sprinkle. Beyond the heavy magnolia soaked with precipitation, I also saw an old black Honda pulling into the Kilpatricks' driveway.

"Who's that?" I enthusiastically tapped Rusty's hairy arm as he looked away from his laptop for only a moment.

"I don't know. Family maybe?" He looked back to the screen and quietly mumbled "hack" under his breath a few times.

I watched a young redhead with an hourglass figure step out of the driver's door. Two shaggy-headed boys hopped out of the back and gathered with her under a bright yellow umbrella. Together they walked to the front porch.

"Rusty, look." I tapped his arm again, not taking my eyes off the trio.

"I see, Tessa. I said maybe they are family," he answered as we both spied out the bay window.

The redhead shook the rain from her umbrella and rapped on the navy blue door. A smiling Baker soon opened it. He reached out and ruffled both of the boy's shaggy heads with his hand. Then he received the bombshell with an embrace and passionate kiss.

I glanced over at Rusty and our wide-eyes locked.

"Or maybe *they* are the reason he killed his wife?"

SIX

It was Wednesday afternoon, but Rusty was back at my kitchen farm table, eyeballing the Honda parked in the driveway across the street as Grace and I drank coffee and discussed yesterday's sordid events.

"He kissed her, Grace, and it was a passionate kiss. It wasn't the way you greet your sister or anything, unless you're from Arkansas."

"There was tongue. I'm sure of it." Rusty grimaced in agreement.

"Baker and that girl were cackling on his back patio so loudly last night that I had to turn the television up to 28 bars so I could hear HGTV! It's not right. It's just not right." Grace shook her head.

"So what do we do? Should we call the police? Maybe we should hire a private investigator?" I suggested.

"No," Rusty said. "I think we need to chill out and think about this. Even if they are lovers, it still doesn't mean he killed Leigh. Maybe Leigh found out about the affair and that's why she killed herself?"

"That's a possibility. If only we had some evidence to point him to Leigh's murder." I bit my lip and tapped my fingers on the table. "We could crack this—"

"Who are you? Jessica Fletcher? You aren't going to solve this case, Tessa," Rusty declared. "Who says there's even a case to solve?"

"You don't appreciate Corey Hart's songs from the 80's but you know who Jessica Fletcher is?" I scoffed.

"I spent a lot of time with my grandmother, and she loved *Murder, She Wrote*. She didn't love synthesizers," he replied. "Let's just keep an eye out and see if anything suspicious deems reporting to the authorities. That's all. I can't even believe I'm here. I should be writing today, not spying on a house and a Honda with two old ladies. No offense, Grace."

"None taken, dear," she said as I became terribly offended that Rusty considered me old. "Those little boys, maybe we could just ask one of the little boys who they are? We could find out if Baker and their mommy are dating."

"Yeah! Kids are stupid," I said. "They wouldn't know we were snooping by asking questions. That's a great idea, Grace! Rusty, if we see the boys come outside, you'll go talk to them."

"Why do I have to do it?" he screeched.

"I'm worried for those kids. Kids shouldn't be living with that psycho!" Grace sipped her coffee as Ellis entered the kitchen.

"Hey! What are you doing here, Rusty? It's not Tuesday." She shuffled over to us while wearing her pink reading glasses with her latest YA mystery in her hands.

"Hey, Ellis," Rusty said. "We're trying to determine if Baker Kilpatrick killed his wife."

"Rusty! She's a child! Don't tell her that!" I scolded him and slapped his hand.

"Oooh, wow, you think the dog doctor killed his wife?" Ellis' eyes grew wide as she turned to look out the large kitchen window.

"No, Ellis. We don't think that. Rusty is clearly on drugs," I sneered.

"Tessa, she might as well know. She's not a baby," Rusty said.

Ellis most certainly is a baby— she is my baby. She may be mature for her age, but she was still a ten-year-old child. However, she's also a mystery lover and this kind of thing was right up her alley. She reads a different *Goosebumps* book every week and grew up with my old *Nancy Drew* paperbacks. I have fond memories of Ellis and her sister both cuddling with me on the couch watching Hitchcock marathons— the same way I did with Nanny. Ironically, *Rear Window* was Ellis' favorite.

"Ellis, we don't know that he murdered his wife. I'm sure he didn't. I'm *certain* he didn't, but we do know that he's got a new girlfriend, which looks—"

"It looks like he got rid of his wife because he was in love with someone else. I get it, Mama. I'm a very mature almost eleven-year-old."

"There are the boys!" Grace interrupted as we watched the two shaggy-headed pre-teens, who appeared to be twins, walk out of the garage and start bouncing a basketball behind the Civic parked next to Leigh's shiny Mustang. They took turns passing, dribbling and shooting the ball at the brick above the garage.

"Rusty?" I asked.

"I'm not going over there to strike up a conversation with those kids, Tessa. That would be creepy. I could be arrested for attempted kidnapping or something. No way!" He shook his head, leaned back in the rustic kitchen chair and folded his bony arms.

"All you have to do is ask if they are new to the neighborhood, maybe talk with them for a minute about basketball and then ask if their mother is dating Baker. Maybe ask how long they've been together. It's so simple."

"Then you do it," he said.

"I'll do it," Ellis volunteered.

"No," I instantly snapped.

"Wouldn't it make sense for me to talk to them? I mean, they look my age." Ellis shrugged.

"I don't think—"

"Tessa, that's a fine idea. You and I will go piddle around in the flower bed while Ellis talks to them. We'll be right there with her. She could clear this whole thing up for us in a few minutes. What if they really are Baker's relatives? There could be a very simple explanation." Grace nodded. "We need to know before we pursue this any further."

"I don't want her going on his property, Grace! He could be a murderer. I mean, remember what he did to your cat?"

"Ellis isn't going to defecate on his lawn, dear," Grace replied and smiled. "I don't want her on his property either, but she can call to the boys and let them walk over here. Let's get this over with and move on. Poor Rusty here needs to be home penning that fascinating novel he was telling me about earlier."

"I don't like this Grace," I argued.

"It will be fine, dear." She reassuringly patted my hand.

It wasn't uncommon for Grace and me to be outside weeding my flower bed or planting impatiens in hers. We both loved gardening and tended to each other's flowers on a regular basis. Several days a week we would stand around in one of our front yards and converse about the clematis climbing the trellis beside my dining room window or the overgrown butterfly bushes on Grace's property. And it wasn't uncommon for Ellis to be perfecting cartwheels on the front lawn as we did this.

What was uncommon was the disheveled 22-year-old hippie in tinted glasses and a Grateful Dead tie-dyed t-shirt loitering on my front porch. Rusty was sure Baker wouldn't recognize him as Ralphie's little brother, but I thought it would be better that he stay inside.

"What if this operation goes nine kinds of wrong and you need me to ninja kick Kilpatrick? I am needed out here with Ellis and you old ladies. No offense, Grace." He grinned as Grace pulled a bendable sun visor from the back pocket of her elastic-waisted cotton capris and placed it on her gray head.

"The vet probably sees Rusty's car over here every Tuesday anyway, Tessa." Grace bobbed her head at his Subaru covered in political bumper stickers that made no sense to me.

"Okay, okay," I conceded. "Rusty, you can stay outside."

Grace and I discussed the thirsty rose bush in my front bed as Ellis did a few cartwheels and then walked to the edge of the plush green yard. Rusty stood with us, rubbed his patchy chin stubble and nodded as if he were enthralled with our horticulture lesson.

"Hey!" Ellis called across the cul-de-sac.

The basketball stopped bouncing and one of the boys called back.

"Are ya'll my new neighbors?" her young voice squealed while she used her little hands to shield her pale eyes from the sun.

"Yeah," one of the boys responded, and they both began to walk down Baker's driveway.

"What are your names?" She asked when the kids reached the edge of our lawn.

The one with the basketball tucked under his arm spoke as I

studied them and concluded that they were definitely twins. "I'm Colin and this is Levi."

"I can't hear them." Grace bent over to pull a daffodil from the black mulch.

"His name is Colin and the other is Levi. The Colin kid is the leader. He's also a punk. I can tell," Rusty mumbled and bit his nails. "He reminds me of my brother, Ricky. That jackleg was always stealing my pot and scratching my X-Box games."

"Will you be going to school here?" Ellis asked.

"Yeah, we'll be in 7th grade," the leader said as he twitched his long hair out of his eyes.

Ellis responded, "I'll only be in 6th grade at the middle school. You'll be over at Jr. High."

Rusty pretended to enthusiastically observe the ferns on the porch while we all quietly continued to listen to the kids.

"Where are you from?" Ellis asked.

"Gulfport," Colin said.

"Is your mom dating Mr. Kilpatrick or something?"

"Joanna isn't our mom. She's our sister," he answered.

"They're in love." The quiet one giggled and made kissing noises.

"How'd they meet?" Ellis inquired.

"She found him on the internet and he came to take care of our sick horse," Colin replied and bounced the ball on the street. "They're getting married in a few months."

"The what? I can't hear. What did he say?" Grace asked.

"The internet," I mouthed. "They met on the internet and they are getting married!"

"The what?" She leaned closer to me gave me a confused glance. "The intelligent?"

"The internet, Grace! The in-ter-net," I loudly whispered.

The warm breeze blew Ellis' sunny hair into her face. "But his wife just died!"

"She shouldn't mention that!" I shrieked as Rusty and Grace both motioned for me to be quiet.

"He and his wife were gonna split up anyway." Colin began bouncing the ball again. "Why has your brother's shirt got a teddy bear on it?"

Ellis turned and looked at Rusty in the Grateful Dead tee.

"That's not my brother," she corrected him. "My mom's helping him write a book. They—"

"Come on, Ellis," I called to her. "It's time to go inside for lunch, dear!"

"That's my mom," she said. "Well, I guess I'll see you guys later."

"See ya." They both turned and walked back to Baker's driveway before Ellis gave a thumbs up and did more cartwheels across the emerald Bermuda.

"They were splitting up anyway, huh? You believe that?" I smirked.

"Not for a second. He probably told that poor young redhead that he and Leigh were going to get a divorce, and then Leigh found out about them. And then—"

"And then he killed her," Rusty finished Grace's sentence.

"Rusty, what changed your mind?" I asked as Ellis switched from cartwheels to back handsprings.

"Those kids are here for the long haul. They're going to school here this year. That's been planned for a while. That's a real commitment. And I know Leigh. She wouldn't kill herself over some guy. She was a tough broad. She tried to set my brother on fire, for Heaven's sake. Besides, I'm a writer. I'm very intuitive," he answered with certainty.

"Would the police open up an investigation if we called them?" I asked.

"I can hear that potbellied Chief Haskins now— using words like *speculation*," Grace scoffed and wiped the sweat from her gray hairline.

"No." Rusty looked to me and chewed on the end piece of his glasses. "Jessica Fletcher, we're going to dig up some evidence. We're not going to give Chief Haskins a reason to use words like speculation."

"Like *Rear Window*?" I clicked my tongue as Ellis joined my side.

"I love *Rear Window*." She giggled.

SEVEN

Jules sat across from me at the dining table on Wednesday evening with a disgusted look on her face as she scraped at the ominous char marks on the tilapia on her plate. Instead of lightly searing the fish, I'd burnt it to a frigging crisp. I was too occupied with thoughts of Leigh Kilpatrick's murder to *lightly sear* anything.

"I'm sorry I burned dinner," I muttered, ashamed, as I reached for the glass of unsweetened iced-tea to wash the scorched taste from my mouth.

"No need to apologize, Mom." Jules shrugged derisively. "It's better than usual. Burning it actually gave it some flavor."

"Jules." Tim shook his head at her.

"What, Dad? I'm being honest. It's, um, what do you say? Blackened? Seriously and disturbingly blackened?" she taunted.

"The stupid fish is burnt, Jules, and I know it." I threw my fork to my plate. "If you don't want to eat it, go to your room and inhale the stash of junk food you've hoarded in your sock drawer."

"Tessa." Tim sighed in preparation for another argument between mother and daughter.

"Well that's what she wants to say isn't it, Tim? She wants to rub it in that her mother, the lame and terrible writer, is also a terrible cook. Right, Jules? Isn't that what you want to say? Go ahead and complain that there's no sugar in your tea, too. I know you want to. I'm sure you've got a 2-litre stored in your room," I sneered.

"Mama," Ellis said with concern.

"Chill, Mother. Maybe you should cut back to twelve pots of coffee per day." Jules rolled her eyes.

"That's enough." Tim poked at the burnt fish and rubbery asparagus on his plate. "Jules, respect your mother. Tessa, calm yourself. Dinner is fine."

I couldn't believe the teenager sitting across the table, maliciously peering at me with angry caramel eyes identical to mine, was my little girl. I couldn't believe our relationship had crumbled in only a matter of months. I couldn't believe that I, the one who brought her into this world and cared for her and fed her and changed her diapers and cleaned her vomit from the carpet, was the bane of her existence. Although I loved her immensely, at that moment, I really disliked her.

"Let's try to have a nice family meal without the two of you bickering. You fight like young sisters," Tim said and unintentionally grimaced at the burnt flakes between his teeth.

We sat in silence and chewed the overcooked protein and washed it down with flavorless tea. I glanced out the dining room window at the Kilpatrick home. Every light in the house was on, and my mind was once again captivated by what was going on behind that navy blue door.

"What did you girls do today?" Tim tried to change the subject.

"I blissfully ate four Snickers bars and a bag of Doritos that I keep hidden in my sock drawer. I washed it down with a gallon of high-fructose corn syrup stored on my closet shelf," Jules sarcastically replied as I glared at her father.

"Jules, you're excused," Tim told her.

"Thank you very much." She stood from the table and left the dining room, her furry companion following closely behind.

"Why do you let her talk to me that way, Tim? She criticizes my book, my meals and my every word. She hates me, and you do nothing to deter her," I said, irritated and hurt.

"She's a teenager, Tessa. This is just a phase—" he began.

"I don't care. You shouldn't allow her speak to me that way." I shook my head. "You just excused her from the table. You excused her from her actions."

"You're right," he agreed and reached for my hand. "You're right, baby. I'm sorry. I'll talk to her."

Tim is the ideal husband and father. He manages to remain kind, compassionate and patient despite all of the estrogen surging in our home. He adores our girls and I know he still loves me as much, if not more, than he did when we met at a toga party in 1997. I also know he supports me as a mother. But the truth is, he's terrified that Jules will resent him, too, if he presses the issue.

"Anyway, so what did you do today, Ellis?" He pushed the empty plate away from him— a plate he'd cleaned solely out of pity and love for his crazy wife, and then wiped the burnt crumbs from his mouth.

"I met the new boys across the street," she innocently replied as I shook my head at her— a signal to zip it.

"What new boys?"

"Mr. Kilpatrick's new family," Ellis said before taking a swig of her watery tea.

"He has a new family?" Tim looked to me.

"He's got a woman and two kids living with him now. They are getting married in a few months."

"They are what?" he asked, shocked.

"I tried to tell you, but you wouldn't listen. I told you something was off with that man. I told you he was celebrating his wife's death. The dirt hasn't even settled on Leigh's grave yet, and he's got some jezebel and her little brothers living with him," I scoffed.

"Wait, what?" Tim put his elbows on the table, confused by it all. "He's engaged to a new woman?"

"I don't know if you could call her a woman," I said. "She doesn't appear to be the legal age to vote. She probably needs a booster seat and still orders from the kid's menu at Applebee's."

"Wow." He shook his head in disbelief. "That's crazy."

"Do you believe me now?" I jeered. "Or do you think my overactive imagination is just running wild as usual?"

"And wait? Ellis, *you* met the boys?"

"Yeah," she said, "Mama and Mrs. Grace and Rusty were outside gardening while I talked to the boys."

"Rusty? Is it Tuesday?"

"No, but he wanted to find out what was going on over at Kilpatrick's place. We saw Baker and the new woman kissing yesterday."

"Ellis, you can be excused, too." Tim's eyes scolded me as he leaned back in the dining chair.

"I'm not done eating." She poked at the burnt fish.

"Go eat a Pop-Tart, honey. It's okay," I said as she sprinted from her seat and eagerly ran to the pantry.

"Ellis shouldn't hear all of this, Tessa. She shouldn't know that the man across the street is celebrating his wife's death, kissing another woman, getting married." He turned and looked out the dining room window to the Kilpatrick house.

"Well, she was bound to find out, Tim. She saw those boys playing ball in the driveway today. She knew he had a new family living with him."

"Still, I don't like it. She's only ten."

"Almost eleven," I mumbled.

He sighed, frustrated with my stubbornness. "So what did they say to her?"

"They said they are going to school in Tupelo this year and their sister and Baker are getting married."

"And you saw them kissing yesterday?"

"While Rusty was here writing, we saw them kissing on the front porch. I'm telling you, it's odd. We think, well Grace and Rusty and I think, that he killed Leigh," I said with certainty.

"Whoa." Tim held up his hand. "Do you hear what you're saying? You're accusing a man of murder, Tessa. Do you know how serious that is?"

"Of course I do, but I think it's true. Rusty and Grace think so, too."

"So you, an old widow woman and a hippie all think he killed his wife?" He looked at me in disbelief. "I'm sorry to disappoint you, Tessa, but that kind of thing doesn't happen around here. It doesn't even make sense."

"A man killing his wife for another woman makes complete sense. Don't you watch Lifetime, Tim, or Hitchcock movies? I'm telling you that the man is a lunatic. He made fun of my organic food and my incontinence."

Tim blinked. "Your what?"

"He saw me holding adult diapers in Piggly Wiggly and was

terribly rude about it."

"What in the world goes on while I'm at work, Tessa?" He threw his hands in the air.

"I told you he was very unpleasant when I first met him. I told you about him celebrating with liquor and happily washing his dead wife's car. I told you all of that, but you don't take anything I say seriously just because I thought Poor Boys Painting slit Mr. and Mrs. Anderson's throats last summer! You pen everything on my overactive imagination, as if that's some sort of disease." I stood from the dining table with the branded fish on my plate and walked into the kitchen.

"Fine, Tessa, don't tell me anything else," he called from the dining room. "Just because a man is getting remarried doesn't mean he killed his wife, but you and Ms. Grace and that hippie writer think whatever you want."

"We will, Tim," I yelled back, my anger getting the best of me. "Now go run to your little hoarding pile of beef jerky and Brach's peanut clusters. I know you keep them in your desk drawer." I threw the terrible meal into the sink and flipped on the garbage disposal switch.

I love my husband. I really, truly love Tim Lambert, and I have been faithful and devoted to him for nearly seventeen years, but just once I'd like him to take me seriously. I'd like for him to believe in my writing, believe in my theories, my opinions, and not talk about my overactive imagination as if it is a fault. I'd like for him to defend me to our daughter, and I'd like for him to take me to the frigging French Riviera.

I decided to sleep on the couch that night.

EIGHT

When I woke the next morning with a crick in my neck from sleeping on the hard sofa, I found a letter from Tim on the coffee table. It simply said, "I love you and your imagination." I didn't know whether to take it as a genuine apology or as a dig at my suspicions about Baker.

I fixed a pot of coffee, pulled out Penelope's story and stared at it for half an hour. Then I scribbled four whopping words: "*I hate this book.*" I left my kitchen and went onto the front lawn, where Grace and I trimmed the daylilies and really tried to refrain from talking about Baker Kilpatrick. We did a fine job until we saw Leigh's Mustang reverse down the driveway, with the redhead at the wheel.

"She's driving her car, Grace," I gasped.

"All right, it's time." Grace tossed the dead daylilies to the grass and rubbed dirt from her hands. "If we want some substantial evidence to present to Chief Haskins– evidence to pin Leigh's death on Baker– the first step is to get some photos of those lovebirds. They spend a lot of time on the back patio. I've heard them every night from my house. Lord only knows what they're talking about back there."

"What are you doing tomorrow night?"

"Let's see, it will be Friday so I'll be watching *Dateline*. What do you have in mind?"

"I'll call Rusty. It's time to crack this case."

On Friday evening, Jules went to a friend's and left a sad Oreo to sit at the kitchen door and wait on her return. While watching the depressed dog shift his gloomy brown eyes around the house, I told Tim I was going over to Grace's house to have coffee and play a game of cards, as I often did since Jack passed away. He and Ellis were sharing a large pizza loaded with nitrates and rubbery cheese, listening to his Van Morrison collection and playing Clue in the living room when I left.

When I arrived at Grace's, I called Rusty. He showed up about

20 minutes later and pulled his dusty Subaru next to Grace's Cadillac parked in her garage so no one, including Tim, would see it. We convened in Grace's living room, adorned with ivory figurines and floral bouquets on every piece of furniture, to discuss our plan.

"I never thought I'd be stuck with two old ladies on a Friday night. No offense, Grace." Rusty pulled binoculars, a flashlight and a rope from his messenger bag.

"None taken, dear." They did their familiar spiel.

"What in the world are we going to do with a rope, Rusty?"

"I don't know. I just know that when someone goes on a clandestine mission, they always have a rope." He held it up and examined it.

"Let's just wait it out for a little while and play a game of Rook. Their lights are on and the cars are home so I'm sure we'll hear them chatting on the back patio soon." Grace walked to her oak kitchen table.

After Grace had beaten us both horribly in an intense game of Rook, we heard the faint noise of annoying high-pitched laughter. The sound reminded me of those girls in my college sorority who drank too many Zimas flavored with Jolly Ranchers and suddenly sounded like cackling hyenas.

"It's time," I said. We stood from the table and walked out the back door.

When we were outside, we definitely heard Baker and his fiery redhead chortling over the chirping of crickets and cicadas.

"I can't see them for the holly hedge." I peered around the corner of Grace's home. "And I can't really make out what they're saying, either."

"We could sneak over by the bushes," Rusty suggested. "It's so dark over there that they'd never see us. I'm sure we could hear them better."

"Yeah, but I want to *see* what they're doing on the patio. We need a photo of them portraying a happy couple." I chewed my lip and thought for a moment. "Okay, Rusty, you go over by the bushes so you can hear, and I'll get a bird's eye view."

"Get a bird's eye view? What, dear? Are you going to climb a tree?" Grace snickered softly and patted her gray curls.

"No, I'm going to climb your roof."

"You're not going to climb the roof!" Rusty exclaimed. "Who do you think you are, Tessa? Jason Bourne? You can't scale a roof. This isn't a Tom Clancy novel."

"Robert Ludlum wrote the Jason Bourne novels, not Tom Clancy," I corrected him. "I just want to see what they are doing. If we want to get some real damning evidence, the first step is to have a photo. I can't see them through Grace's wall of shrubbery."

"Then get a photo of them from your kitchen window tomorrow. You're too old to climb the roof, and I'm not going to do it. I'm terrified of heights," Rusty argued.

I looked at him, mouth agape. "Just how old do you think I am, Rusty?"

"Let her climb the roof, son. Jack's ladder is in the garage." Grace patted Rusty's arm. "It will be fine."

Rusty shifted his eyes from Grace to me several times, then sighed and reluctantly agreed.

"Great, so I'm in charge of photos and Rusty, you're in charge of eavesdropping by the hedgerow," I gave orders.

"What will I do?" Grace asked.

"Jack was an avid outdoorsman, wasn't he, Grace?"

She nodded.

"Do you still have his camouflage clothes? That paint he wore on his face when he went duck hunting? Maybe some walkie talkies?"

"All of his hunting stuff is still in the spare closet. You need all of that?"

"Yeah, and I'll need a spoon and that jar of organic peanut butter I gave you last week."

"Why do you need that?" Rusty asked.

"I don't know how long I'll be up there."

Rusty perched Jack's 20 foot ladder against the back of Grace's house. After I doused my complexion in black face paint and put on pants that were nearly a foot too long and two feet too wide, I prepared to ascend. My expensive camera with the extra-long lens hung from my neck, and the walkie talkie and organic peanut butter that I'd purchased Grace last week (in an attempt to wean her off the poison known as Jif) were tucked somewhat securely in my pocket. Gathering the large pants tightly at my waist with one hand, I carefully climbed with the other.

"I still don't understand why you're dressed like that," Rusty scoffed.

"I can't play a covert spy in Under Armour shorts and a tank top, now can I, Rusty? Duh," I said as I scrambled up the latter.

When I reached the top, I took a few deep breaths and quietly scaled the shingles in my New Balance tennis shoes. As I crawled to the highest point, I kept telling myself not to look down. I finally reached the tallest gable and was relieved that I had the perfect view of Rusty army crawling toward the dark hedge. I could also clearly see Baker Kilpatrick's back patio.

He and the redhead sat close together in lawn chairs and sipped from brown bottles of beer. The porch light illuminated them grinning at one another like old lovers.

I pressed the camera with the large lens to my face covered in war paint and undoubtedly saw him stroking the girl's arm. Then I focused the camera on an upstairs room and saw both boys sitting in game chairs and staring at a large television screen showcasing PlayStation soldiers dressed in camouflage and running through a jungle. As I admired the cartoon soldiers' flawlessly applied face paint, I stealthily pulled the walkie-talkie from my pocket.

"Grace," I whispered. "Grace, come in."

"I'm here, dear. What do you see?" She spoke quietly from 25 feet below on her own porch with her cat, General, tucked under her arm.

"They are really close. Oh, wait. He's leaning in. They are kissing, Grace! Major spit swap!" I gave a play-by-play.

"Do you see Rusty? Is he in position?" Grace asked.

I looked for scruffy Rusty lying in the grass by the hedgerow, but it was too dark.

"I can't see, Gracie, but hopefully the eagle has landed and he's within earshot. I'll stay up here a while and get some good photos of the murdering beau."

"Okay, dear. Be safe."

"Over and out, Gray Goose." I put the radio back in my pocket.

I snapped a few clear photos of the couple making out in the Adirondack chairs. Then I tried to relax and get as comfortable as any woman could on a steep roofline in 85 degree heat and a dead man's size 2x hunting attire. I secured myself by pressing my tennis shoes into the gable, and I pulled the organic peanut butter, sans hydrogenated oil, from the inside pocket of the camouflage pants. I dug into the jar with a plastic spoon and ate.

I watched Baker and his girlfriend flirt and giggle. I occasionally looked over to my own house to make sure Tim or Ellis weren't coming to retrieve me from the "card game". The rest of the street was dark, but I did use the camera to zoom in on Dr. Parker's home. I vaguely saw an orange spark of fire on the upstairs balcony, followed by a haze of smoke that rose to the street light. I'm sure the cloud wasn't attributed to Dr. Parker, but rather his sons. I'm also sure that cloud wasn't attributed to anything manufactured by Marlboro. I let the camera hang from my neck and continued to snack.

I dug around in the peanut butter jar with the plastic spoon for a few minutes until I saw the redhead leave her chair and sit in Baker's lap. She took a swig from his bottle, grabbed the back of his neck and sucked his rugged face in ways that should only be broadcast on Showtime after midnight. The moon came out from behind a cloud at that moment and cast a shadow on Rusty lying still as a snake and trying to peer through the bushes to witness the perversion.

With the spoon sticking out of my mouth, I tucked the peanut butter jar under the crook of my arm and reached for the camera hanging from the neck strap. As I brought it up to my eye, the BPA-free plastic jar slipped and went tumbling down the roof.

"Tessa, come in! What's that?" Grace soon called over the walkie talkie in my back pocket.

I didn't have time to grab the radio before she spoke again. "I was almost hit in the head by a jar of organic peanut butter. And you said the Jif was going to kill me!"

As I stretched for the walkie-talkie in my back pocket, my foot slipped. Suddenly I was sliding down Grace McKinney's steep roof in her dead husband's camouflage with a spoonful of peanut butter sticking out of my mouth and the strap of the heavy, rattling camera choking me.

I began rolling to the right so I would land in the grass instead of plummeting 20 feet to the concrete patio below, killing myself and Grace (and her cat) in the process. As I tumbled, I picked up speed and wondered how I would explain to Tim that I'd broken my neck during an innocent Rook game. Despite grabbing for the gutter, I slid right off the roof. Grace's overgrown hydrangea bush caught my fall. Thank goodness.

"Tessa!" I heard Rusty's raspy voice as he quickly army crawled toward me, but I couldn't answer. I just lay in the bushes—stunned, out of breath and covered in pink petals.

"Tessa? Dear?" Grace whispered loudly, peering over me with a flashlight in her hand.

"Vanessa?" I heard another voice, and I immediately knew it belonged to the same douchebag who'd ridiculed my faux-incontinence at Piggly Wiggly.

A flashlight shone on my face covered in black paint and the Canon camera strap tangled around my throat. The large pants hung halfway off my body and the peanut butter spoon stuck out of my mouth.

"Hey, everyone." I mustered a small smile. "There's nothing to see here. Move along."

Rusty and Grace both reached down for me in the bush and helped me to my feet. After removing the camera from my neck and pulling up the oversized pants, I then took the cracked spoon out of my mouth and saw a hydrangea petal stuck to it.

"What are you doing?" Baker grilled as the redhead clung to his side.

"I was… um…" I stood there, floundering.

"Stealing cable," Rusty interjected.

"What?" Baker looked to Rusty.

"She was trying to rig up some cable and steal it for the old woman. No offense, Grace," he said.

"What do you know about stealing cable?"

"I don't. This guy here does." I pointed at Rusty. "But he's terrified of heights. I was trying to run the cable through the roof and into the attic, but I slipped."

"What?" Baker eyed me like I was an idiot.

"Do you know a better way to steal cable, Baker?" I smirked as if *he* was the idiot.

"Why are you dressed like that? You look like a hunter."

"So I wouldn't be seen. Duh!" I cocked my head. "Didn't you hear that the cops are really cracking down on cable theft around here? I was just taking precaution," I fibbed.

"What's the camera for?" the redhead quietly chimed in.

"I wanted to take photos of the installation to show this guy so he could confirm that I was doing it correctly." I glanced at Rusty.

Baker looked to Rusty, and I could tell he was trying to place him.

"Do I know you?" he asked and eyed Rusty's dingy, hippie clothes.

"I don't think so." He shook his head. "Unless, hey– did you do time with me at Jackson Correctional?"

Baker scoffed.

"Oh, Mr. Kilpatrick, please don't tell anyone. I'm just a poor widow woman. I just wanted *Cat Fancy* channel. I can't afford all of those upgrades with Tupelo Cable Company. Please don't mention this to anyone," Grace pleaded in a feeble voice.

"What a bunch of fools. Come on, Joanna." Baker pulled the red head by the arm.

"Who's the girl, Baker? Baby sister? Granddaughter?" I picked another piece of mulch from my messy hair.

"No, this is my new girlfriend. And yes, I'm aware my wife has only been dead for three weeks. And no, I don't care what you or anyone else in this town thinks about it." He smirked and stomped out of Grace's yard.

Grace, Rusty and I all sighed in relief as Baker and his girlfriend walked away. They helped me limp to the back porch and go inside.

"Are you sure you're okay? I'll fix you some water, dear." Grace assisted me onto the couch. I threw the huge pants to the floor and welcomed the air on my legs sticking out of jogging shorts.

I ran my hands across the scrapes on my knees and realized I was still holding the peanut butter spoon. "Get this thing away from me. I nearly choked to death on it during the fall," I said as I threw it at Rusty.

"So," Grace said as she entered the living room and handed me a glass of ice water, "what did you hear, Rusty?"

"You'll never believe it." He shook his head in shock and sat on the floral couch.

"What?" I sipped the water as Grace and I both sat wide-eyed across from him in matching pink high-back chairs.

"Clear as day, I heard him say it. I heard him say, 'I'm so glad she's gone and we can finally be together.'"

"And what did she say?" Grace sat on the edge of her seat as her cat weaved between her white SAS sandals.

"She agreed and said she wished it hadn't taken so long for Leigh 'to get out of the way'!" Rusty slapped his knee with the spoon in his hand. "What's that sound like to you?"

"It sounds like they had been plotting to get rid of Leigh." Grace pursed her lips and shook her head in disgust.

"What else? You were over there for at least fifteen minutes. What else did you hear?" I asked him.

"Well, just a bunch of flirty stuff. I couldn't make out a lot of what they were saying. They were whispering in each other's ears and kissing, but they are definitely glad she's gone," Rusty replied.

"That's definitely detrimental, but it still doesn't mean he killed her though, does it?" I sighed. "We need more evidence."

"Maybe, but we aren't letting you climb any more roofs, Tessa." Grace observed a gash on my ankle.

I looked out Grace's living room window at the Kilpatrick home. "I don't know how we'll do it, but we've got to get inside that house."

NINE

Dr. Pulaski's clinic was incredibly posh. A concierge walked around the waiting room and offered people aloe-covered tissues, Slush Puppies, cough drops, fresh donuts and coffee. I never accepted any of the foodstuffs because I thought it was disgusting to eat in a waiting room where germs were rampant and invisibly breeding on every bite.

There was even a "movie theater" connected to the waiting area. It wasn't really a theater— just a small, dark room packed with folding chairs and a big-screen TV that played old stuff like *Oliver and Company* and *Titanic*. When I had the flu last year, I tried to watch Leonardo DiCaprio going down with the ship, but the lady sitting behind me was coughing up so much lung butter that I ran for the door. I didn't want to catch her pleurisy on top of my flu.

The receptionist also handed out pagers that would blink and vibrate when the nurse was about to call you back to see the doctor. Those things were pointless. Pagers worked in a crowded Olive Garden while you waited outside on a bench, unable to hear the hostess call your party, but the clinic was small, never crowded, and the nurse still loudly called your name anyway. It seemed like a waste of AA batteries to me.

The nurse took my vitals as I waited on Dr. Pulaski to enter the small examination room. He finally opened the door, with hair white as fresh snow and a Gorbachev-like birthmark on his forehead. I always wanted to ask him if he'd ever thought of concealing it with Maybelline.

"Well, Tessa, what brings you in today?" He sat on the small rolling stool and looked at my chart.

"I took a nasty fall on Friday night and now my back is hurting pretty badly." I rubbed the sore spot above my hip.

"Like last time after playing powder puff?" He grinned.

"Yeah, exactly like that."

"Well, your last MRI showed bulging at L4, so it's probably inflamed. How'd you fall and hurt yourself?" He stood and walked over to me.

"I was stealing cable for the old lady next door. I fell off her roof," I answered bluntly.

"You're not serious, Tessa?"

"I'm afraid so. You know Sugar Creek Cove is a pretty rough hood. We're always stealing cable, buying Schwan's meals on bad credit, using our sprinklers even when there's a water shortage in the height of summer. We've got a lot of rebels on our street." I winked.

Murderers too, I thought.

"Tessa," he said and chuckled. "Your stories never cease to amaze me."

I frowned in pain as he pressed the tender spot.

"Do you still have the exercises I gave you for strengthening your core and your back? That will help with the inflammation." He backed away from me.

"Yes sir, I've been doing the exercises. I'm taking fish oil for inflammation. I'd just really like a cortisone shot. Those always work."

"Did the Percocet help last time?"

"No, please, Dr. Pulaski," I pleaded. "I can't go through that constipation again. It made me mean as a wet cat. Tim nearly filed for divorce."

He laughed heartily.

"Can't I just have the shot?" I begged.

"I guess that'll be all right. I'll send a script for Percocet over to Rexall just in case, okay? Just rest and ice as much as you can. Vickie will give you a cortisone shot." He wrote in my chart.

"Dr. Pulaski, may I ask you a question?"

"Sure," he answered as he continued to scribble.

"I'm working on a new novel and need some medical expertise."

"That's exciting! What do you need, Tessa?" He smiled.

"Well, the protagonist in the book is killed by her husband."

"Oh, it's a mystery. Keep going."

"But he wants to make it look like she committed suicide. How do you think he would go about doing that?"

"Well, I don't know," he answered then paused. "He could feed her an overdose I guess?"

"Yeah, that's exactly what I was thinking. You don't think that's too far-fetched?"

"Well, you're the writer. Do you think it's too far-fetched?"

"I was thinking he could get her drunk on liquor, right? And then pour a bottle of sleeping pills down her throat after she passed out. How does that sound? I mean, that would definitely look like suicide. That would kill a person, wouldn't it?"

"It wouldn't be good for a person, that's for sure. If she were drunk enough, she wouldn't know what he was pouring down her throat. Enough sleeping pills and sauce would kill an elephant. Sounds like a best seller to me, Tessa."

"That's how I'm going to do it. Kill her off, I mean. If you think it sounds realistic?"

"I think so," he agreed. "There are a lot of sick-o's in this world. I'm sure it's been done before."

I'm sure, I thought.

"Now don't go telling Mrs. Pulaski the plot twist. I want her to buy it when it's published, all right?"

"All right, Tessa. Good luck with the novel." He got up and headed for the door. "Vickie will be in with your shot soon."

As I waited on Vickie with her heavy blue eye shadow and hot pink Lee Press On nails to shoot steroids into my hip, I was convinced that Dr. Pulaski had just helped confirm Leigh Kilpatrick's cause of death.

TEN

After I received the shot and rested on the couch for a while, I looked out the mudroom door and saw Jules sitting on the wicker patio chair, scrolling through her phone, as she waited on Oreo to defecate in his favorite spot beneath the riverbirch tree. I opened the back door and stiffly walked down the cobblestone steps to her.

"Hey," I called as the warm wind signaled that a summer storm was on the way.

"Hey," she said, dryly, and began to stand and leave.

"Just stay there, please. I'd like to talk to you for a minute," I told her as she rolled her eyes and sighed in disgust that I was within 100 feet of her.

"What?" she huffed over the sound of Oreo's collar jingling in the distance.

"I want to apologize to you for the other night." Fidgeting at the pain in my bulging disc, I leaned over the back of a lawn chair. "I shouldn't have yelled at you at dinner. I was mad I burnt the fish, and you were certainly out of line with your sarcasm and disrespect, but I should have been more mature about it. I shouldn't have been ranting and throwing my fork around like a crazy person."

She said nothing.

"Well? Is there anything you want to say to me?"

"No," she replied sternly as both anger and sadness at our deteriorated relationship bubbled within me.

"Jules, what have I done to you? We've always been close. Do you remember the trips we took to Moo Moos for ice cream cones after preschool at the Baptist church? Reading Junie B. Jones books for hours in your bed? It wasn't that long ago we'd get our nails done and try to decipher Mandarin. Remember I thought the nail tech said I had a big toe the size of Godzilla's?"

She stifled a grin.

"Hey, I know you aren't a little girl anymore, but you're still my girl. I love you more than anything in this world, Jules. I want us to be close again. I want to talk to you without you rolling your eyes or making me feel stupid. Do you really think I'm lame and stupid?" I asked.

She shook her head and quietly picked at her nails.

"Well…" I paused. "That's all I wanted to tell you. I love you."

She ignored me and whistled for Oreo. He ran to her, jumped into her lap and they stood and passed me. When the door closed behind Jules, I rubbed my eyes in frustration until I was interrupted by the sound of a garbage can rolling to the street.

I straightened my aching back and sluggishly walked to the corner of the house, peeking around the brick to see Baker Kilpatrick walking up his driveway after leaving his trash on the curb. An idea came to me. I winked at the imaginary light bulb above my head and went inside.

"How's your back?" Ellis asked as she watched the television on top of the refrigerator and ate her nightly Pop-Tart with a glass of organic hormone-free milk.

"The cortisone shot helped, but I'm still kind of stiff," I answered while taking the overflowing garbage bag out of the kitchen can.

"Why does it flare up like that?"

"Overexertion I guess." I shrugged. *Playing football. Falling off an old woman's roof while taking photos of the murdering neighbor.* "Ellis, ask your father to bring the garbage downstairs. He's in his office."

"Yes ma'am." She hopped down from the stool and disappeared to the back of the house.

As I was emptying the wastebasket in the downstairs bathroom, Tim appeared with the trash from upstairs.

"I'll get it." He reached for the small can. "How's your back?"

"It's okay. I can take it out."

"I will take it out. Just go sit down and rest."

"No, I'll take it," I insisted. "I want to run over to Grace's for a minute and see if she has a better ice pack than that old thing in our freezer. I used it in my diaper bag fourteen years ago to chill my breast milk."

"I don't think you need to *run* anywhere," he joked.

As Tim tossed the upstairs trash into the big can in the garage, I saw junk food wrappers through the transparent sack from Jules' room. I hadn't always been a *health nut* (as Baker had called me), but after seeing a documentary on Netflix about chemical-laden food a few months ago, I just wanted my family to eat healthy. My passion to feed them kale hadn't seemed to deter Jules, though. She had friends smuggle red dye and high-fructose corn syrup into our home like cocaine at a women's prison.

I wheeled the big green can down our driveway, despite Tim insisting that he would do it, and then I shuffled like the hunchback of Notre Dame down the dimly lit cove and went to Grace's front door.

I rapped on it shave-and-a-haircut style so she would know it was me instead of a serial killer. A few seconds later, her porch light turned on and moths swarmed to it. She stood before me in a hairnet and cotton nightgown covered in daisies.

"It's nearly 9 o'clock!" She stepped aside so I could come in.

"I need to borrow an ice pack." I flinched and rubbed my back.

"Are you okay? Did you take the Percocet?" she asked with concern as she walked to her freezer in the kitchen.

"Lord no, Grace. I can't handle a week of constipation. I'm fine. Just a little stiff."

She handed me the cold gel-filled bag. "Well that's what happens when you fall off a roof."

"It's garbage night which means Baker's can is on the street."

"Oh, Tessa." She gave an unfavorable sigh. "What do you hope to find in the man's garbage?"

"Why do you sound discouraged, Grace? We all think he killed her, don't we? Isn't the garbage can the perfect place to find discarded evidence?" I asked as we walked back to her foyer.

"Tessa, dear, I do think he's a bad man. I wanted to get a photo of him with the new girl, and I was okay with Ellis talking to those boys and you scaling the roof, but when you fell and we almost got caught, I rethought the entire situation. This is a serious accusation, murder."

"But Rusty heard them talking about getting Leigh out of the way. Remember? We can't stop now!" I exclaimed.

"I just don't think it's a good idea, Tessa. I don't think we need to pursue this any further. If he is a murderer, do you really want him to catch you searching through his trash? You're liable to end up like his wife. I can't bear to watch you wheeled out on a stretcher."

"Everything will be fine. I'm going to do this, Grace," I said adamantly.

She half-heartedly nodded, her wrinkled face covered in disappointment, as General purred next to her fuzzy peach slippers. "I don't guess I can stop you if you're going to steal his garbage."

"I'm going to steal his garbage," I confirmed.

"And how are you going to steal his garbage, dear? The street light is right in front of his house. He's liable to see you, a hunched over and limping woman, slowly dashing away with his can."

"I'm going to casually switch my can with his. Then I can roll it into my garage and look through it after Tim goes to sleep," I said. "Maybe I should borrow Jack's hunting—"

"And after you steal his garbage? What's next? Are you going to plant a bug in his home?" She groaned.

"I've thought about it. What about one of those microphone pens or teddy bear nanny cams?"

"Go home and get some rest, honey." She patted my shoulder. "We'll meet by your begonias in the morning. Maybe we can send the photos taken from the roof to Haskins tomorrow."

"Good night." I exited the home that smelled of lavender and moth balls.

On the slow walk back to my house, I nonchalantly grabbed Baker Kilpatrick's large green garbage can and wheeled it over to my driveway. I pulled my identical can over to his curb, walked back across the street and went inside.

Tim had been sawing logs for a good 45 minutes while a *Cheers* rerun played on the television, and I quietly slipped out of the bed. Wearing an old California Raisins t-shirt and plaid sleeping shorts, I put on my flip-flop house shoes and shuffled to the garage.

The garage door squeaked loudly as it opened, and I prayed it wouldn't summon my family to investigate. When the coast was clear, I sprinted in the light summer drizzle as fast as I could (which was the equivalent of a newborn foal walking) and lugged Baker's rolling garbage can up my driveway and into the garage next to my Tahoe. After shutting the squeaking door, I pulled the Hefty bags from the canister and drug a folding chair from the corner. Then easing my stiff back into the chair, I sat beneath the dim light and tore open the first sack.

Judging by the amount of sugar products I found in Baker's garbage (cookie and snack cake packages, several empty 2-litres of Pepsi, frosted cereal and three empty bags of actual sugar), I'm surprised the man isn't diabetic. I put the empty food cartons, old light bulbs and paper towel rolls in a pile until the first bag was completely empty. I was discouraged that I hadn't found anything significant.

I ripped open the second sack of garbage and found more sugary packages and normal stuff– Ziploc bags, empty beer bottles, napkins, straws and junk mail from Publisher's Clearing House. I even found a couple of things addressed to Leigh, but nothing of importance– a credit card offer and invitation to a 5k sponsored by the hospital where she had worked.

When I reached the bottom of the second bag, I discovered some shredded pieces of paper damp with backwashed beer. I pulled out a tiny blue piece, another blue piece, a larger white one, a portion with the number 7 on it. I gathered all of the bits of paper into a small pile next to an oil stain on my garage floor and began putting them together like a puzzle.

It was a photo of the ocean with an incredibly long bridge suspended across it. The words "7 Mile Bridge to Key West" framed the top. It was a postcard.

I turned all of the parts over, at least 20 of them, and pieced them together so I could read the words scribbled on the back.

Baker Kilpatrick
428 Sugar Creek Cove
Pontotoc Springs, Mississippi 38288

Baker, I can't wait to have you here with me.
Please get in touch with me soon.

Heart,
Leigh

The post date was June 28.

Five days ago.

LEIGH

I can't believe I agreed to hide in this place. I can't believe, with my abhorrence of sweat and cats that I agreed to come to Key West, Florida to wait for Baker.

I told him I wanted to leave the country. I told him I wanted to go some cold place on the other side of the world. I was so sick of Mississippi heat, heat in general. I'd spent my entire life drenched in Southern sweat. Yakutsk. Yah-kootsk. I said the word over and over again in my mind. That's where I should have gone. I could be wearing a stylish fur hat while sightseeing and listening to Rosetta Stone's Russian Edition. Yakutsk: cold and clear on the other side of the world.

But, for some God-forsaken reason, Baker has always wanted to live in Key West. And Lord knows you can't argue with Baker Kilpatrick. If you do, you're liable to get a swift kick to the face with one of his size 13 Doc Martens that he wore in high school. He once banged me over the head with those clodhoppers merely because I suggested that he throw the 20-year-old worn-out shoes in the Goodwill pile.

But Baker loves me. I know he does. He didn't have to help me disappear. He didn't have to help me get out of the mess that I created for myself. He could have let everyone find out what I had done. He could have let them drag my name through the mud and throw me behind bars. He could have let the toothless drug dealer in Birmingham slice my throat or harass us both for the rest of our lives. He could have let all sorts of horrible things happen to me, but he didn't.

Instead, he let me kill myself.

ELEVEN

I couldn't go back to sleep after finding the postcard. I tried, but I tossed and turned for an hour before getting up to brew a pot of coffee. I chugged caffeine and paced the kitchen relentlessly. Then I threw on a poncho to protect myself from the pounding rain, and I hobbled outside to switch the garbage cans back to their proper homes.

After taping the postcard together, I spent the next hours guzzling more coffee and wishing I could call Grace or Rusty to tell them what I'd discovered. A phone call to Grace at midnight would scare her to death, and I'd see Rusty in the morning, so I just sat at my kitchen table, re-reading the card and waiting on sunrise as the summer storm raged through Pontotoc Springs and headed straight for Tupelo only a few miles away.

When I heard Tim coming down the hallway the next morning, I quickly stuck Leigh's note into the catch-all drawer and replaced it on the kitchen island with Penelope's story.

"Babe, have you been working all night?"

"All night," I quickly answered. "Yes, *alllll* night."

"Did you have a breakthrough?"

"Yes, I did. I had a serious breakthrough. Yes, all night."

"Tessa, are you okay? You're talking awfully fast." He bent down to me sitting on the barstool and examined my bloodshot eyes.

I sounded like some sort of dope fiend, wired on caffeine, as I scratched my messy hair and fidgeted with my hands.

"Coffee. I've had so much coffee, Tim. I think I'll clean the baseboards." I nodded excitedly while he stared at me like I was mad.

"Are Andrew, Darcy and the boys still coming tonight?" Tim walked to the refrigerator.

"What?" I asked.

"It's the 4th of July, Tessa. Hamburgers. Fireworks. Freedom. Are they still coming?" He drank straight from the apple juice carton.

"Oh, that, yeah, that, yeah, that will be fine," I stuttered.

"What time?"

"I don't know Tim." I shrugged and stood from the table. "I

better go get dressed. Rusty will be here at 10."

"He's coming today? It's a holiday." He frowned.

"Writers never have the day off." I hurried out of the kitchen.

Soon before Rusty arrived, Tim, Jules and Ellis left to run errands and spend a small fortune on fireworks and food for the cook out.

"Tessa, I came up with a serious plot twist last night," Rusty excitedly proclaimed as he entered my kitchen door and threw his messenger bag on the table. "What's wrong with your eyes? They're bloodshot. Have you been smoking pot? Did you go through my bag last week and find my stash?"

"I've been drinking pot—pots and pots of Folgers, Rusty. You'll never believe it."

"No, *you'll* never believe it. Listen to this! What if Artie tries to kill Cody before the race because, *get this*, he's in love with Mary?" He clapped his hands and grinned like a Cheshire cat. "Artie is in love with Mary! Who would see that coming?" I rolled my bloodshot eyes at him.

"Rusty, sit down. I have to show you something." I pointed to the kitchen chair.

"Tessa, can we focus on this for a moment? Think about it. Artie is secretly in love with Mary. What if he and Cody get into a fight over her? What if Cody has to burn him in the eye with his Camel to defend himself from Artie's knife to the throat or something? See!" He snapped his fingers excitedly. "He could be saved by cigarettes after all! Yes!"

"Sit down and look." I pulled the Scotch-tape covered postcard from the drawer and handed it to him.

"What is this garbage?"

"It's just that. It's garbage. It's a postcard that I found in Baker Kilpatrick's garbage."

"You found it in his *what*? Why are you handing me a torn and taped post card of the 7 Mile Bridge you found in Baker's garbage?" He tried to hand it back to me.

"Turn it over and read it! Read it!" I pushed it back to him and sat down.

Rusty quietly mouthed the words on the card.

"Leigh? Kilpatrick?" He looked to me, stunned.

"Check out the date, Rusty. Check the frigging postdate on the card!" I stood again from the table and paced the kitchen.

"Five days ago? Oh my God, Tessa, Leigh Kilpatrick is still alive?"

"It seems so." I smiled. "It certainly seems so!"

"So who was the dead woman they pulled out of his house?"

"That is the million dollar question, Rusty, my boy. *That's* the million dollar question."

The idea of Cody and Artie vying for Mary's love was put on the backburner as Rusty and I discussed the postcard at length. *What? How?* And most importantly, *who* was that dead woman on the stretcher? We abruptly ended the conversation and Rusty drove off in his grimy Subaru when my family arrived home with a rack of ribs and enough pyrotechnics to light up Yankee Stadium.

My beautiful sister, Darcy, was soon walking through my kitchen door with her dishwater blonde hair swinging over her tan shoulder. Her adoring husband followed her, toting dishes of her famous coleslaw, strawberry salad and chocolate pie.

"Happy Fourth of July!" Her contagious smile lit up the room.

"Happy Fourth of July!" I reached out and hugged her.

She took over my kitchen as her husband, Andrew, and Tim shook hands and immediately began their familiar argument about college football. We were devoted to Mississippi State and Andrew, born and raised in Tuscaloosa, preached Crimson Tide.

"Where's Evan?" I asked as Darcy put the strawberry salad in the refrigerator.

"He's spending the holiday with his girlfriend's family at their cabin in Muscle Shoals."

"He's old enough to do that?"

"He's seventeen, Tessa. My baby boy is seventeen!" She shook her head in disbelief.

My other two handsome nephews, Drew and Mason, soon walked through the door and showered me with hugs. Then Mason, the youngest, headed straight for Ellis' room upstairs. Ellis and Mason were only months apart in age and had always loved one another like siblings.

Although Tuscaloosa was only two hours away from Tupelo, my sister and I rarely saw one another; with the exception of holidays and birthdays. We used to frequently spend weekends together and go on trips to Gulf Shores during the summer, but Darcy was so busy now with her catering business. I was busy, too, spending most of my time working on the stupid novel and writing articles and trying to solve missing person cases. Sadly, we'd drifted apart over the years. We made an effort to speak on the phone a few times a week, but I missed my sister. I was always ecstatic when we were together. It was a comforting and homey feeling to have her near.

We sat at the back patio table and sipped on Blue Moons while I sliced the cantaloupe. Oreo barked and chased Ellis and Mason as they did cartwheels across the lawn, and Jules and Drew, the teens, sat in the swing beneath the massive oak and compared phone apps. The husbands manned the grill and continued their sarcastic jabs at the other's favorite SEC team.

"How are things with you and Jules?" Darcy rocked in the patio chair and braided the long hair hanging over her shoulder.

"She's fourteen, Darcy. She hates me."

"You know Evan and I went through the same thing. He hated me for the longest time. Dad was the good guy. I was the bad guy, but he outgrew it. She'll outgrow it, too. You know she loves you," Darcy encouraged me.

"I just don't know. I *always* disliked Mom, but I never had this kind of resentful relationship with Nanny. I don't know if this is normal. I have friends who have great relationships with their teens. I just don't understand what I've done wrong." I angrily tossed the cantaloupe into the bowl.

Because our mother turned into a complete fruit loop when our father passed away, Nanny and Papa Ellis were the only real parents Darcy and I had ever known. Our mother's parents had both died when she was young, so we never met them. She had a handful of brothers and sisters scattered around the country, but they never reached out to us when dad passed away and mom lost her mind. We didn't really know anything about her side of the family. But Nanny and Papa eagerly offered to take us in as our mother sat silent on the couch and stared at the wall for years, and they always said it was the best decision they ever made.

"Trust me, it is perfectly normal, and you haven't done anything wrong. She's trying to find herself and thinks you are standing in her way. She'll see she's mistaken. She's fourteen, Tessa, and she's an idiot. We may not have ever have been disgusted with Nanny, but I assure you, we were both idiots in other ways when we were fourteen."

"She loves you, Darcy. When you arrived, I noticed how she clung to you and didn't want to pull away. If I so much as touch her, she shivers with disgust."

"That's because I'm not her mother." Darcy sipped her beer. "Do you want me to have a talk with her before I leave tonight? Maybe she'll confide in me."

"No, just leave it be." I shook my head.

"Okay." She shrugged. "I finally answered the phone when Mom called last week."

"Are you going to take her to Georgia?" I grinned.

"I'd rather pluck my toenails off with pliers, Tessa. She infuriates me to no end. She didn't ask about me or the boys or anything. As soon as I said hello, she recited her famous line."

"I need," we said in unison.

"Gosh, I miss Nanny and Papa." I sighed as Darcy agreed.

Our grandparents often talked about our dad, their only child, because we had so few memories of him. Their stories and photos portrayed him as a kind, decent, hard-working man who loved his girls with all of his heart. We knew that if our dad was anything like them, he was definitely a good man. We also knew we'd been blessed to have him, even for a short while.

Nanny died first, suddenly, of colon cancer when I was 25. I was devastated by the loss. I spent many days and nights paralyzed with grief at her absence. And then Papa went only nine months later, and it seemed too much for my heart to bear. For a few months, I feared that I'd go crazy like my mother– confined to a recliner, eating frosting from a can, extensively dating the "Mississippi Misfits", unable to leave my home. By the grace of God, though, I managed to pull through.

The doctor said Papa died from clogged arteries, (years of barbeque and a gallon of sweet tea per day) but Darcy and I knew his true cause of death was a broken heart. He just couldn't go on living without Nanny.

"You remember those peach preserves Nanny made?" Darcy smiled. "I can still see her canning on that rickety screened porch while Papa spit chewing tobacco in an old tin coffee can. I think about them every day."

I did, too.

"Mom mentioned her new boyfriend. Tick."

I cringed. "His name is Tick?"

"I guess so. She said his name as if it was normal, like she was saying Dave or Robert. She said, 'I'll just have to see if my boyfriend Tick can take me to Georgia. At least he loves me.'"

"Shouldn't we be proud?" I rolled my eyes.

When our bellies were full of pork and night finally fell, Grace came over to sit with Darcy and me on the front lawn in Adirondack chairs while the husbands and kids lit up the night sky with bottle rockets and shower makers. As I watched Ellis and Mason chase one another with sparklers, I could hold my tongue no longer.

"I told you about the lady across the street, Darcy? Leigh."

"Yeah, that's so sad," Darcy answered and studied the Kilpatrick home while Grace and I exchanged a glance.

"Grace and I thought her husband killed her," I said.

"What? Why?" Darcy exclaimed.

"Very suspicious stuff going on over there, dear." Grace took a bite of the chocolate pie on the paper plate in her hand.

"He has another woman and some kids living over there. Leigh has only been dead for a few weeks and he's already moved on," I replied over the popping of firecrackers.

"That doesn't mean he killed his wife, Tessa," Darcy told me.

"No, he didn't kill his wife." I looked to Grace. "We thought he did, but we were wrong."

"We were wrong? He didn't kill her?" Grace questioned, confused, as sweat dampened her gray hairline.

"Look at this." I pulled the folded and ratty postcard from the pocket of my navy blue shorts. "I found this in his garbage can last night."

"Wait, you're looking through the man's garbage?" Darcy frowned at me.

"And scaling my roof for photos," Grace tattled as I nudged her to be quiet.

"Tessa—" Darcy began.

"Read it." I passed the postcard to Grace as she sat the paper plate of pie in her lap. Darcy leaned over her shoulder and they examined the card together by the bright light of the rockets.

"What?" Grace gasped. "She's alive? Leigh Kilpatrick is *alive*? She's in Key West? Florida? She's in Florida?"

I nodded quietly.

"Tessa, I don't think you should be digging through that man's garbage. I don't think you should be involved in this—" Darcy steadfastly scolded me in her "big sister" way.

"So who did we see being wheeled out on the stretcher last month? I can't see much with these 68-year-old eyes, but I definitely saw a dead body come out of that house," Grace declared. "I'm sure of it."

"I don't know, Grace, but I intend to find out."

"No, Tessa." Darcy grabbed my arm. "You need to hand this over to the police. I don't want you involved in this. It could be really dangerous."

"Rusty and I were talking this morning. We can't call the police yet. What? Are we going to give them a torn postcard and some photos I snapped on an old lady's roof? No offense, Grace."

"Offense taken, Tessa," Grace pouted.

"We've got to get one more piece of evidence."

"Dear, this is no longer a murder case. Leigh is alive, and we've got plenty of evidence to suggest an investigation. This post card alone is enough," Grace said.

"This most certainly *is* a murder case. Remember the dead woman wheeled out of the house?"

"You can't—" Darcy began.

"Darcy, I don't want you telling Andrew about this. He'll surely tell Tim. Those two are thick as thieves, unless they are talking about football. Tim will discourage me the same way you are. I am not going to get into any trouble with this. I will contact the cops, but we need more information."

"You aren't going to get into trouble? How do you know that, Tessa?" Darcy smirked.

"I know because Rusty and I came up with a solid plan."

TWELVE

I sat in the scorching hot parking lot of the hospital and examined myself in the rearview mirror. Amazing how a pair of scrubs can transform a crazy woman with writer's block (and trying to solve a cul-de-sac case) into someone who looks like she accurately knows how to take blood pressure.

When I was browsing for the perfect pair at Scrub Wear House yesterday, I have to admit that I felt somewhat silly. Was I really doing this? I thought about backing out several times as I approached the register with a powder blue uniform. My thoughts were interrupted by my friend Cameron, a dental hygienist, when she asked what I was doing there. I rattled off some cockamamie story about shopping for a Halloween costume. Surprisingly, she didn't question my sanity although it was July and it was a known fact that Tim and I always went to the annual Halloween party at Becky Davis' as Robert Palmer and one of the guitar-toting models from his video, "Addicted to Love."

I got out of the Tahoe and went inside the bustling hospital. I expected to possibly be stopped at the door by an overweight security guard in a starched shirt and ill-fitting polyester pants, but no one gave me a second glance. I looked like a legit nurse. I looked like I belonged there.

I took a few turns, passed the admissions desk and walked through the cafeteria until I was in the administrative offices wing. Keeping my eyes to the floor, I passed countless hospital personnel. When I found the sign for the medical records room, I immediately noticed the badge access keypad on the wall. I knew swiping a badge to enter the room was a possibility, and Rusty had suggested I take Dr. Parker's badge from his unlocked Jaguar, but I wasn't a thief. I may have been a wannabe detective, but I wasn't a thief.

Miraculously, a Godsend stepped out of one of the offices and into the empty hallway. It was an environmental services employee pushing a cart of cleaning supplies, and he was walking toward me.

"Excuse me?" I smiled. "Dr. Leland Parker asked me to access some medical records for him while on my lunch break, but I seem to have left my identification badge in my locker. Would you mind swiping me in?"

I expected this man in scrubs, permeating the faint scent of bleach, to question my motives. I feared that he'd seen enough crime dramas to know that a woman who "forgot" her badge and batted her eyes while asking for help was probably a liar. I was prepared to karate chop him in the neck, use his identification to gain access to the medical records room and then drag his limp body and hide him behind a file cabinet until he regained consciousness, but he didn't question me at all. Instead, he gladly scanned his badge next to the keypad and the heavy bolt on the door unlocked.

When I was in the large, fluorescently lit room lined with shelves, cabinets and a wall of computers, my head grew dizzy. I didn't even know where to begin. Would I find what I needed on the shelves, in the cabinets, or was everything electronic? I'd never been in a medical records room before so this was all foreign to me. However, I was intelligent enough to know that most records are filed by last name, so I passed the row of computers and went to the "K" shelf.

As my heart pounded and I saturated the new scrubs with nervous perspiration, I frantically scoured the shelves. There was no sign of Leigh's records. I decided they must have been deemed for older files, so I went to the closest computer and sat down on a rolling stool.

The screen didn't prompt for a password, so I assumed granting access through the badge swipe was enough clearance. There was a flashing cursor next to "Last Name", and I typed in "Kilpatrick".

Several Kilpatricks appeared, including Baker James, but I only clicked on "Kilpatrick, Leigh Anna" and began to read. I glanced at the door every few seconds in fear that someone would enter, possibly Dr. Parker, and I'd spend the rest of my life in Guantanamo Bay.

Suddenly my phone rang and vibrated in the pocket of my scrubs. I anxiously retrieved it to see my mother's name on the screen.

She only called when I was in the middle of something important (like posing as a nurse and hacking into medical records). I ignored the call and threw the phone back into my pocket.

A certified, scanned copy of Leigh's death certificate appeared on the screen. Cause of death was attributed to "suicide by overdose." Someone was dead on arrival that June morning and examined by Dr. Raji Manthram.

So if Leigh Kilpatrick was in Key West, then who the heck was dead?

As I exited the medical records room, confused by the death certificate of a woman who wasn't dead, a doctor in a white coat greeted me at the door. He smiled at me in a very non-suspicious way, but as I always do when I'm nervous, I caught a bout of diarrhea of the mouth.

"I left my badge in my locker," I said, already wishing I'd shut up. "I had an environmental services guy swipe me in. I had to pull some medical records for Dr. Leland Parker. He's a neurosurgeon. The best in the state, I hear."

The older gentleman looked at me strangely.

"Yes, I know Leland," he replied.

"He's a great guy. He gives the best Christmas presents to his staff. And what about those three adorable boys he has? They listen to classical music. Dr. Parker says it makes them smart. That wife of his must listen to classical music, too. She's a scientific genius," I muttered as I backed out of the room and sprinted down the hallway.

I feared I'd handled that as smoothly as a container of cottage cheese. I feared the doctor in the white coat was going to call out, "Quick! Someone stop that woman!" and suddenly my light sprint turned into a full-force marathon run. I flew down the hallways and through the cafeteria like a frigging cheetah. I was no longer inconspicuous, shouting "excuse me" when I caused one nurse to drop a stack of papers and another to spill her coffee. I hoped everyone who watched me dart through the hospital assumed I was a really important medical person headed to a code blue, whatever the world that meant. I was only familiar with the term because of *Grey's*.

When I ran out the main exit and the scorching July heat consumed me, I clutched at the pain in my side. I hadn't run like that since college, and my body was seriously confused and angry. I bent over for a moment, caught my breath and then casually walked to my Tahoe.

"Rusty," I spoke into the phone as I turned the ignition and warm air from the AC blasted my face, "someone was really brought into the hospital and assumed to be Leigh Kilpatrick."

"You accessed the medical records?" he asked surprised. "You really did it?"

"Yes, I saw her death certificate."

"Hmmm." Rusty clicked his tongue as if he was in deep thought.

"Dr. Parker said—" I began.

"That's it," he interrupted me. "What if Dr. Parker is in on this? He's the one who told you she died. What if he made the whole thing up? What if he was working with Baker? What if he created a phony death certificate, had people pose as EMTs and wheel her out of the house? What if he's involved?"

"No." I refused to believe it. "Dr. Parker wouldn't."

"He has the access, Tessa. He would be the perfect guy to help stage her death."

"But *why* would she stage her death?" I rapped my fingers on the warm steering wheel.

"I have no idea, but Baker may not be a bad guy at all. He could have asked Dr. Parker to help stage her death in order to *help* Leigh. We aren't trying to solve a murder now. We're trying to figure out why Leigh Kilpatrick faked her death and ran off to Key West. She didn't disappear for funsies. She must've been in real trouble."

"Okay, let's assume Dr. Parker helped phony her death. Let's assume he and Baker were only helping Leigh by sending her to Key West. The death certificate showed that she was examined by Dr. Raji Manthram. Is he in on it, too?" I watched the busy parking lot around me.

"That name doesn't even sound real, Tessa. Dr. Parker could have–"

"He is a real person. Tim saw him in the ER when he had kidney stones." I remembered Tim shrieking in pain like a little girl.

"Well, maybe he's in on it, too. Maybe the whole hospital knows Leigh is in Key West. Maybe we are the last to know!" Rusty sighed in frustration.

"No," I demanded. "There's more to this story. I really believe someone died in Leigh Kilpatrick's house that day. I'm going to find out who it was. I'm going to find out why Leigh is in Key West. I bought scrubs, Rusty. I'm already too invested in this."

On the drive home, my head continued to swim with thoughts of Leigh Kilpatrick sitting on a southern beach. Was Baker really a good guy? Had he sent Leigh away to protect her from something? Was Dr. Parker really involved? What in the world happened to our boring country cove?

When I pulled into the driveway, I was met by Ellis running toward my car with her arms flailing. My heart immediately began to pound when I saw the terror and the tears in her eyes.

"Mama!" she shouted as I hurled the SUV into park.

"What is it?" I frantically threw open the door.

"Something is wrong with Oreo!" She wiped snot from her nose. "Dr. Kilpatrick is with him in the back yard!"

She pulled on my arm and I chased her up the drive. This was the second time I had run– really run– in less than an hour. I felt the side-stitches returning. My bulging L4 disc certainly wasn't too thrilled about all of my activity for the day, either.

When we reached the back yard, Baker and Jules were kneeling over the black and white Lhasa Apso beneath the aged oak tree. Jules looked up to see me rushing toward her, and tears the size of quarters began falling from her caramel eyes. She stood and quickly walked to me.

"Mama!" she bellowed. "He won't move. Something's wrong with him!"

Jules buried her head into my shoulder and sobbed. I hadn't been this close to her in months, and although I was brokenhearted to see her so devastated, it was bittersweet to hold her. I ran my fingers through her almond-colored hair and tried to calm her.

"Look at me." I pried her messy head from my chest. "It's going to be okay. Tell me what happened. Why didn't you call me?"

"I just sent Ellis inside to call you. I let him outside to go to the bathroom and he cried out and then collapsed. I didn't know what to do so I ran over to get the vet," she cried as I wiped her soaking cheeks.

"Okay, come on." We walked to Baker.

"Snake bite." Baker examined the limp dog's neck. "See the puncture wounds?"

"Oh Lord!" I rubbed Jules' back as Baker spread apart the black hair on Oreo's neck and revealed fang marks.

"I need to get him to my clinic as quickly as possible." Baker scooped Oreo's frail, fuzzy body into his arms. "There's still a chance the antivenin could work. Follow me."

Baker hastily scurried across our yard, into the street and carefully put my daughter's best friend in the passenger seat of his BMW. Jules, Ellis and I frantically climbed into my Tahoe and sped behind him.

I was terrified Oreo was going to die on the 15 minute drive from Pontotoc Springs to Baker's clinic in downtown Tupelo. I stifled the tears and tried to remain calm and positive as Jules wailed in the passenger seat and her baby sister hugged her neck from the back.

When we reached Baker's veterinary clinic, he leapt from his car with the dog in his arms and swiftly unlocked the door. He ordered us to sit in the waiting room while he and Oreo disappeared to the back.

Tim had a real estate closing that afternoon, so I sent him a text message explaining the situation and told him to come to Baker's office when he was done. Jules rested her head on my shoulder and whimpered while we waited for over an hour.

The sign on the door indicated that the office was closed on Wednesdays, so I couldn't help but feel grateful to Baker Kilpatrick for doing all of this on his day off. I'd been accusing the man of malicious things for a month. I'd fallen off a roof while spying on him. I'd hacked into his wife's medical records only hours earlier, and now he was administering antivenin to my daughter's dying dog. Guilt began to mix with all the other emotions I was experiencing.

I was holding Jules under one arm and thumbing through an issue of *Dog Fancy* when Baker opened the door to the waiting room.

"Okay," he said and sat down beside us. "I think we got to him in time. I did blood work and thankfully I had copperhead antivenin on hand. He's got an IV of that, antibiotics and pain meds going right now. He's already showing some signs of improvement."

Jules cried out with relief.

"He's going to be critical overnight, and I'll need to stay up here to monitor him, but he's got a pretty good chance. If we'd wasted any more time, I don't think we would be as lucky."

"Baker," I spoke through my tears. "I can't thank you enough for this. I know this was your day off. We are so glad—"

"You don't owe me any thanks, Tessa," he said compassionately. He was kind, considerate, caring and he even called me by my correct name.

"I don't want you to worry, Jules. I'm going to do everything I can to make sure Oreo is up and running again soon, okay?" He patted Jules' shoulder.

"Thanks, Dr. Kilpatrick." She wiped her puffy face.

I was stunned. Was this really the same man who kicked Grace's cat? Was this the same man who acted like such a douchebag in Piggly Wiggly? Was this the same man who scoffed at me for helping an old widow woman obtain free cable? Was this the same man who moved a young vixen into his home only weeks after his wife was presumed dead? Did he suffer from multiple personality disorder? Was he psychotic? Was he such a kind man that he helped his wife stage her death in order to keep her safe? Good *and* evil must have shared a home behind those beady eyes.

"Thanks, Baker." We stood from the vinyl waiting room chairs. "What do I owe you?"

He shook his head. "Don't worry about that right now. Just go home and try to enjoy the rest of your day. I'll let you know how he progresses."

I picked my jaw up off the floor and the girls and I went home.

Baker kept in contact with us throughout the night as he monitored Oreo. The next afternoon, he personally delivered the groggy (but stable) dog to our door step, along with a bill that didn't tally up anything close to what it should have. He hadn't charged us for the antivenin, which Google had led me to believe would be nearly $1200 a vial.

Jules was so thankful for Dr. Kilpatrick's help that she hugged his neck. I felt uneasy that the man who I'd been accusing of murder was holding my daughter in his arms, but I managed not to pry them apart. Jules truly was grateful for what he'd done, and I could see in Baker's squinted eyes that he was sincerely glad he could help.

I wrote Baker a check, insisting we should owe him more for saving our dog's life, but he refused. I caught a hint of annoyance in his tone when I continued to press the issue, so I decided to just pay him what he'd charged.

I watched Baker walk down our driveway with the check in his hand as Jules took the patient up to her room to care for him, then I retrieved the taped postcard from the catch-all drawer and studied Leigh's words again.

THIRTEEN

On Friday evening, Rusty, Grace and I convened around her kitchen table as she threw the smack down on us in Rook again.

"I'm just so confused," I said and reached for a handful of pretzels in the Tupperware bowl on the table. "I had no idea there was a compassionate bone in his body."

"I think it's time to let this go." Rusty studied the cards in his hand. "Leigh isn't dead. Baker isn't a murderer. He's a dog-saver. There's nothing left to investigate."

"There's plenty to investigate, Rusty!" I exclaimed. "She may not be dead, but her death was faked for a reason."

"And that's not our business." He glared at me. "I should be writing about Cody and Mary right now. Not still discussing the Kilpatrick drama and playing Rook with two old—"

I cut him off. "I'm 38. I'm not old."

"I'm just as confused as you, dear, but I think Rusty is right. Leigh is gone, but she must be gone for a good reason I bet. I think we've let our suspicions get the best of us," Grace replied.

"So much stuff still doesn't add up." I sighed. "Who was the woman on the stretcher?"

"Isn't it obvious? It was Leigh, Tessa. She was probably wheeled into an ambulance that Dr. Parker set up to arrive, and she was taken to an airport or a bus station," Rusty stated.

"But her face was blue," I argued. "Grace and I both saw how lifeless she looked. I think there were specks of vomit on her chin."

"That could've been makeup, Tessa," Rusty groaned. "Haven't you seen *The Walking Dead*? You think those are real zombies?"

"But why go through all the trouble? Surely Dr. Parker didn't arrange for her to be picked up by an ambulance just so we would see her. It doesn't make sense!"

"I've seen a lot of things in my day that don't make sense, Tessa," Grace said.

"I repeat. It's time to let it go."

"No," I argued. "I can't just let this go. I feel it in my gut that something about this isn't right. I still want to plant a bug in the house. I just want to hear—"

"Count me out." Rusty shook his head and stood from the kitchen table. He walked to the refrigerator and grabbed a can of Coke.

"Please, Rusty, just help me do this last thing. Help me get a bug in the house. We'll only listen for a few days. Then I'll let it go. I promise," I pleaded.

"No." He drank from the red can.

"Oh, come on. Aren't you the least bit curious about what is said in that house?"

"I'm not," he said. "Tell her she's being crazy, Grace."

"Well," she said as she patted the gray curls around her face, "maybe it wouldn't hurt to listen for just a few days."

I nodded at her with encouragement.

"What? I thought you were with me on this, Gray Goose. What good can come from listening to their conversations?" Rusty leaned against the kitchen counter. "We're liable to get caught and be thrown in prison. I can't do time. Do you have any idea what they'll do to a hippie like me in prison?"

"Eavesdropping could clear this up in a second," I urged him. "And then I'll let it go, I promise. We'll get back to your book, think of fresh new synonyms for cough and everything will be back to normal again. No more scaling roofs or playing Rook with old ladies. Please, Rusty?"

"I've had some crazy friends in my day, but you two old ladies are the craziest."

On Tuesday morning, Grace and I anxiously watched from my kitchen window as a clean-shaven Rusty Ballard pulled his mother's pewter Caravan up Baker's steep driveway. He stepped out of the driver's seat, pushed the wire-framed glasses up his nose and wriggled around in his khaki pants and white dress shirt. Rusty walked to the side of the van, slid open the door and pulled out a Rainbow vacuum.

"He looks good cleaned up." Grace sipped from her cup of Folgers.

"I hope she lets him inside," I said, biting my lip as he walked up the porch carrying the bulky vacuum cleaner.

Joanna opened the front door and Rusty began smiling and chatting. After a few seconds, she nodded and opened the door wider for him to go inside.

"Bingo!" I forcefully grabbed and squeezed Grace's hand.

Forty minutes later, the navy blue front door opened and I summoned Grace from the living room where she was sitting on the couch watching HGTV. Rusty exited the house without the vacuum cleaner. He smiled and waved at Joanna while walking to his mom's van.

"Holy crap, she actually bought the thing!" I exclaimed as Grace joined me at the window.

"Tsk. Naïve girl," she scowled.

Without paying us old ladies at the window any mind, Rusty reversed down the driveway and sped out of the cove. Moments later, my phone rang.

"Can you believe I actually sold her on that thing? I've unloaded more vacuums in an hour than my brother has in a month. This may be my calling!" I could tell Rusty was smiling.

"Congratulations," I said. "The bug? Where did you put it?"

"I stuck it under the kitchen table. Call the number I gave you to see if it's working," he replied. "It won't ring or beep or anything to alert her that you are calling in. We can listen in and everything is also being recorded on the flash drive. The thing cost a fortune at Radio Shack, and I expect you to reimburse me for at least half."

"Yeah, yeah," I mumbled. "I'm going to call in now. Thank you, Rusty."

"Don't say I never did anything for you. Now start brainstorming cough synonyms," he said before ending the call.

I called the number assigned to the listening device and could clearly hear Joanna singing loudly and off-key with Lady Gaga on the radio. It was working. It was really working.

I went about my day, editing Penelope's dialogue, dusting the living room and folding laundry, while listening to the speakerphone. Joanna was watching an episode of *Maury* as I steamed the broccoli for supper. I was so disappointed to learn that there was a 99.98% chance that Marcus was *not* the father.

When Tim arrived home, only minutes after Baker, I switched off the speaker and propped the phone between my shoulder and ear. I pretended to talk to my sister. Motioning for my family to go ahead and eat their healthy meal, I excused myself to the bedroom and continued listening to the neighbors.

Baker spoke kindly to her, the same way he spoke to my family when Oreo was about to meet the White Light. He and his new girlfriend flirted and laughed at the other's silly jokes. He didn't get angry when she told him she bought an incredibly expensive vacuum from some nerd with glasses. For a brief moment, I was jealous of their rhetoric. It had been ages since Tim and I spoke to one another so excitedly and so in-love.

"Is everything okay?" Tim poked his head in the bedroom.

"Yeah," I answered from the bed. "Mom wants us to take her to Georgia again. Tick can't leave the state. Judge's orders."

Tim rolled his eyes and left me alone to go eat supper with our girls. I continued to eavesdrop on the couple across the street.

I knew I couldn't pretend to be on the phone for the entire night, so I sent Rusty a text to let him know that it was his shift. He would listen in until my family was asleep.

I stood over the stove and ate a hormone-free pork chop and cold broccoli. After I'd cleaned the kitchen, I walked through the living room to discover my family on the couch watching a Hitchcock movie on TCM. Jules held a sore Oreo in her lap and rubbed his ears. Ellis rested her head on her dad's shoulder and propped her bare feet beside his on the ottoman.

"*Rear Window*. My favorite." I sat between Jules and Tim.

As Jimmy Stewart focused his camera on Raymond Burr cross the courtyard, Jules leaned against my arm. She was close enough for me to smell her coconut-scented hair. I was in heaven.

When we'd finished watching *Rear Window* and half of *Vertigo*, the girls retreated to their rooms. I nudged a snoring Tim on the couch and sent him to bed. Then I changed into my pajamas and sent Rusty a text. He replied that he hadn't heard anything of importance, so I dialed in.

I spent an hour sitting on the couch and working on an article for Gabriella about rekindling relationships with your teen. All I heard through my speakerphone was silence. I was disappointed that Baker and Joanna must've been away from the device, which was planted beneath the kitchen table in the open-floor plan. Finally, though, I heard the sound of their voices drawing closer.

"I just don't understand, Baker!" Joanna's tone was low, but stern. *"What do you mean she's not dead?"*

My heart leapt from my chest and my eyes grew wide. I tossed the laptop to my side, gripped the phone to my ear and stood to pace the living room.

"Okay, sit down." He sighed over the sound of a kitchen chair sliding across the floor. "I'll tell you everything."

"Yes, yes, yes, yes," I squealed with excitement and suppressed the urge to urinate on myself.

LEIGH

I'm sitting on a rooftop café overlooking Duval Street, eating a dish of lobster gnocchi and drinking a mojito. A relative of one of Hemingway's six-toed cats keeps weaving between my legs. I hate cats and always have- ever since I was a little girl and my wretched sister brought one home that she found in a dumpster behind the gas station. It hissed at me and clawed at my face, leaving a bloody gash on my cheek. Every time a cat darts in front of me or rubs their whiskers against my leg, I remember that demon-possessed hairball and have to remind myself that I'm doing this for Baker. I'm here– battling felines and scorching heat and incessant Latin music– for him.

I could still be in my large home on Sugar Creek Cove, with the love of my life, if it weren't for Eliza Studstill. Eliza Studstill walked into North Mississippi Med pharmacy at the very moment I was emptying a bottle of Oxycontin into the pocket of my Snoopy scrubs. I can still see her, with her fat round cheeks and doe eyes, asking what I was doing in that maddening voice that resembles Fran Drescher's.

She swore she wouldn't tell, but I knew she would. And later, I knew for certain she had. I saw the way the other nurses looked at me when I walked by, the way they whispered in the break room and at the nurse's station. I watched them silently mouth the words, "thief" and "pill head." I knew it was a matter of time before Eliza Studstill's little secret about me was all over North Mississippi Med, and I knew it was just a matter of time before an investigation was underway and it was discovered just how many pills I'd taken over the years. I knew it was simply a matter of time before I was sitting in some court room, probably thrown into some dingy jail cell, never allowed to nurse again.

I lay all of that blame on Eliza, but the other trouble I had brewing like a hurricane in the Gulf wasn't her fault. It wasn't her fault that I had a cocaine habit I couldn't afford. It wasn't her fault that a ruthless and toothless drug dealer in a Cadillac Deville threatened Baker and me if we didn't pay him the hundreds of thousands of dollars I owed him. I took responsibility for most of that. Well, I took *most* of the responsibility. It was my sister's fault that I was on coke in the first place, the same way it was her fault that cats gave me nightmares. She'd thrown both the drug and that mangy feline in my face.

Baker and I could have dipped into savings and paid Mack the drug dealer, but once his debt was null, we knew he wouldn't just go away. Mack wasn't the type of guy to just go away. He'd keep harassing us. I couldn't get clean with scum like Mack living and breathing because he wanted to keep me hooked. He wanted me to be in debt to him. If we paid him and I went back to rehab, he'd be waiting on me as soon as I got out, like always. He drove from Birmingham to Tupelo weekly just to wait on me in the hospital parking lot to remind me of the money I owed and keep me hooked on powder.

Baker was brilliant. He always had been. He could look at an animal and immediately tell what was wrong with it. When he looked at me for the first time, high and out of my mind, walking half-naked down a street near Elvis' birthplace in Tupelo, he knew what was wrong with me. And he loved me anyway. He took me in and tried to clean me up, and so what he knocked me around when I was out of line? I deserved it. He was just trying to save me.

It was his brilliant plan that sent me here, with the cats and the heat. He said we'd stage my death, and I would come here and stay clean, although it is so hard to do. There's more cocaine coming in from Miami to Key West than there is in all of Mississippi or Alabama. But because I love him so much, I haven't touched the stuff once in 42 days.

He said I would wait here. He'd come and we'd start a new life. Mack would think I was dead, Baker would pay him, and he'd forget all about me. Eliza's accusations wouldn't mean a thing anymore. We'd live down here, 90 miles from Cuba, and we'd have a fresh start.

There are so many single men down here in Key West. Tanned by the heat I hate so much, but mysterious and attractive and rich. One is smiling at me now across this rooftop café. He looks like the type to take me dancing and keep me high. He looks like the type to show me a good time, but I casually flash him the diamond on my left finger as I drink my minty mojito. He nods and looks away.

I'm here in this hot hellhole that's crawling with cats for Baker. I'm turning down other handsome men for Baker. I'm staying sober solely for Baker. That's how much I love him. I cannot wait for him to return to me.

FOURTEEN

Joanna and I both sat in speechless awe at Baker's words. Leigh Kilpatrick had fled her life here in Mississippi; she'd fled a dangerous drug dealer and a potential life in prison. Our quiet country cul-de-sac had become the setting of one of those Hitchcock masterpieces that I watched so often.

"I can't go to Key West now, Joanna. I love you. I don't want to lose you," Baker whined.

"This is just…I can't," she stammered with shock.

"I'm just not going. She can stay down there alone for all I care. I'll get in touch with her tomorrow and tell her. I'll finish paying off her drug debt and let Mack continue to believe she's dead, but I'm not leaving you," he said adamantly.

"You really think she's going to accept that you aren't coming, Baker? She'll come back here. She'll bring that drug dealer with her! She's a loose end!" Joanna exclaimed in a hushed voice, as not to alert her little brothers.

"I know. I know!" I envisioned him pacing his kitchen.

"I just don't understand, Baker. She had a funeral, didn't she? Who was in the casket? How did you fake her death?" she quietly pleaded for answers.

"How did you fake her death, Baker?" I repeated.

He gave a long and loud sigh, followed by quiet. Joanna and I both grew impatient with his silence.

"Tell me!" she demanded. "Was the casket empty?"

"No," he grumbled.

I stopped pacing my living room and pressed the telephone firmly against my ear.

"Who was it? Who was it? Who was it?" I whispered.

"The less you know−" he began.

"Who was in the casket, Baker?" Joanna demanded.

"Who was in the casket, Baker?" I demanded.

"It was no one of importance," he said.

Then my butterfingers accidentally dropped the phone—at the

worst possible moment. It fell from my hand and banged against the hardwood floor. I scrambled to put it back to my ear and was greeted with quiet. The call must've ended when it fell, so I mumbled expletives and hurriedly dialed the listening device. It didn't connect, so I tried again. On the fourth try, as my hands shook with anxiety, I could finally hear Baker's voice.

"She was just too drunk to know what we gave her. She was dead in an hour. It was that simple," he finished.

"NO! What was that simple? Who was it?!" I gritted my teeth in anger.

"This is unbelievable, Baker!" I could picture Joanna shaking her auburn head. "This is too much."

"I know. I'm so sorry, baby. I'm so sorry I didn't tell you the truth. I thought Leigh would just stay away and not try to contact me, but she keeps sending postcards. I just knew you would find one. I couldn't keep lying to you. I wanted you to hear it from me before she called or showed up at the door or something crazy. I'm sorry for all of this, but I'm going to make it right," Baker pleaded with Joanna.

"So what *are* you going to do? She'll come back here when she knows you aren't coming for her."

"She can disappear as easily from Key West as she did from here. I can't go through her drug addiction again. I can't get wrapped up in her drama and trouble with the police and Mack. I can't be forced to pay anymore of her debt. I can find someone down there to take care of her. I know people," he said with certainty.

"You're talking about getting rid of her? *Killing her*?" Joanna whispered.

"Yeah," he said. "I killed her off once, didn't I?"

Baker and Joanna soon left the kitchen and all was silent. Stunned, I ended the call and immediately dialed Grace's landline. I didn't care that it was after midnight and she would lurch from the bed with her heart pounding in her wrinkled chest. I could not keep this secret all night.

"Hello!" Grace frantically shouted into the phone.

"Calm down, Gracie. It's just me. Everything is okay. It's Tessa." I shielded my mouth with my hand so Tim and the girls wouldn't hear me from the quiet of their beds.

"Oh for Heaven's sake, Tessa! You scared me to death! I was sure my nephew was in jail again. Do you know what time it is?" she scolded me.

"I couldn't wait to tell you what I heard, Grace. This is heavy. Major."

"Well what is it?"

"Baker told Joanna that Leigh is in Key West. She fled down there after getting in trouble at the hospital for stealing pills. She owed some drug dealer hundreds of thousands of dollars. That's why she faked her death. She's in Key West waiting on Baker." I peered down the hallway to make sure none of my family members were approaching.

"Oh! Good Lord! You heard all of that?"

"That's not the heavy part." I shook my head.

"There's something heavier than our drug addict neighbor faking her death?"

"We did see a dead body being wheeled out on that stretcher, Grace."

"Well, who in the world was it?" She nearly shouted.

"I don't know. I dropped the phone before he revealed her identity. When I could hear them again, he was saying how simple it was. They got someone drunk and she was dead within an hour. They killed someone, Grace. I don't know who it was, but Baker Kilpatrick is a murderer after all!"

"Come on. It's late, Tessa. You dropped the phone and only picked up the end of the conversation. Surely you..." she stammered.

"Lillian Grace McKinney!" I exclaimed. "I'm absolutely certain of what I heard! Baker Kilpatrick is a murderer!"

And then my dear, precious 68-year-old, gray-headed, widowed neighbor, in her shock and surprise, spouted off a string of curse words that would make George Carlin blush in his grave.

"Well, you've got to send Rusty back over to get the recorder. We have to send it to Haskins tomorrow. You can't get any more proof than that, Tessa! The man confessed to murder!"

"He is planning a hit on Leigh, Grace. He's going to have someone in Key West kill her. We have to warn her."

"He's going to what?" I feared this was all too much for ole' Grace.

"He told Joanna he was going to get rid of her. He said he knows people. We have to tell her!"

"We don't have to do any such thing. Get the confession to Haskins. He can warn Leigh. Our job here is done!"

"What if they don't get to her in time, though? I can't live with that kind of guilt. I have to warn her. I have to do it tomorrow. I've got to catch a flight to Key West tomorrow." I began brewing a pot of coffee.

"This is ludicrous, Tessa. You can't possibly believe you can go down there and warn her quicker than the authorities can handle it."

"Tomorrow is Wednesday. Baker doesn't work tomorrow. Rusty can't go over there and get the recorder back with Baker at home. The plan was for Rusty to go back on Thursday and pose as the salesman again, claim that he forgot to give Joanna a free attachment to the vacuum and sneak away with the recorder and the flash drive. That was the plan, Grace. Leigh could be dead if we wait to get the evidence to Haskins on Thursday. I have to go tomorrow," I argued with her as piping hot coffee dripped into the Bunn pot.

"Goodness gracious, Tessa. How in the world are you going to convince Tim to let you fly down to Key West tomorrow to tell our neighbor, who is supposed to already be dead, that she's about to be dead? He'll never let you go." I could tell Grace was out of her bed and pacing her home. I heard the faint sound of her fuzzy slippers sliding across the hardwood.

"I'll think of something to tell him, but I am going to Key West. Tomorrow."

FIFTEEN

By 4AM, the coffee pot was empty and birds began chirping outside my kitchen window. I'd spent hours chugging caffeine and explaining everything to Rusty over the telephone. He was adamant about attempting to retrieve the recorder even though Baker would be home on Wednesday, but I was unyielding on going to Key West to warn Leigh. He finally called me a crazy old lady and hung up the phone. I booked a noon flight from Memphis to a connector in Atlanta. I'd be in Key West by 4:30 PM.

I crawled into the bed to catch a few hours of jittery rest before Tim left for work. Soon the sound of his razor banging against the side of the bathroom sink woke me from unsound sleep. I snuck up behind him and wrapped my arms around his chest.

"Well, good morning." He smiled at me in the mirror, his face half-covered in shaving cream.

"So, I had a breakthrough with my book last night." I rested my face against his back.

"That's great," he said before dragging the razor across the stubble.

"I decided to change the setting. I will never be able to visualize the French Riviera." I let go of him and sat at the vanity stool. "I'm going to change it to Key West."

"That's a great idea." He rinsed the razor in the sink. "Can you remember much about Key West, though? We haven't been in what, 13, 14 years?"

"I remember a little." I gulped, then added, "But I thought I'd go back."

"That would be fun. I'd like to go back, too. Maybe we can plan that over the girls' fall break? A family vacation?" He glanced at me in the mirror.

"Yeah," I said, "but I thought I'd go back sooner than that. I thought I'd go back, well, today."

Tim wiped his damp face with a hand towel and gave a hearty laugh.

"My flight leaves at noon." I looked at my hands and picked at the peach nail polish on my thumb.

"Tessa, are you serious?" He turned to look down at me sitting on the paisley stool. "You're just going to fly to Key West? Today? In what"– he glanced at the clock– "five hours? Were you going to tell me and the rest of your family?"

"I'm telling you now." I looked up to him with desperate, puppy-dog eyes.

"Tessa..."

"I'll only be gone a day or two, Tim. I've just got to do this. This book is eating me alive. The writer's block, the mind constipation, is putting a strain on all of us. Don't you want me to move on from this story? Five years I've wasted on this book. I need the inspiration. Hemmingway, Tim! I need Hemmingway!" I whined and tried to conjure up a few tears.

He stood over me in his white Hanes t-shirt and plaid boxer shorts, rubbing his smooth chin and shaking his head for a few moments. Then his face softened and he gave a reluctant sigh.

"Okay, I understand. I understand you need to do this," he said as I cheerfully stood and wrapped my arms around him. "We'll make it a family vacation. I can sneak away for a day or two. I wanted to skip a vacation this summer to save a little money, but it might be good for all of us to get away and rest."

"No!" I pulled away from him. "I have to do this on my own. This isn't a leisure trip. It's a business trip. I have to concentrate on this book. I'm not going down there to rest. I'm going to work. Please, Tim."

"I..." he stammered. "Why can't we–"

"Just please understand." I took both of his hands into mine. "I have to do this on my own. Today."

"Okay," he said, looking into my brown eyes and exhaling. "I can work from home and stay with the girls while you're gone."

"If you have a showing or go somewhere for more than a few hours, just let Grace know. She'll be glad to help with the girls. She'll be checking on you." I let go of his hands and headed to my closet.

"Are you sure this is what you need to do?" he called from the bathroom.

"I'm absolutely certain!" I pulled my rolling suitcase from the closet shelf.

As I tossed clothes into my bag, I explained the situation to my sleepy girls. I knew Ellis would be supportive, as always, but Jules' reaction was a pleasant surprise. Instead of riddling off, "I told you so's" about the much-needed setting change, she enthusiastically smiled and approved of Key West as the new location. She brought me the manuscript from the kitchen drawer and even hugged me for a full ten seconds before I reversed my Tahoe down the driveway and headed to the Memphis airport.

Both flights were uneventful, with only a small amount of turbulence and, thankfully, no fat, sweaty man with B.O. occupied the cramped seat next to me. I thought about Leigh Kilpatrick incessantly until I pulled my manuscript from my bag. I read over it, noting that Key West really could work for the setting, as I ate four bags of peanuts and chugged a bottle of water. Finally the plane out of Atlanta landed, and I was engulfed in the warm, salty air of Key West, Florida.

I'd made a reservation online at a bed and breakfast on Truman Avenue. A cab driver (who drove his yellow mini-van that smelled of plantains faster than Dale Earnhardt, Jr. on Dexatrim), dropped me in front of the beautiful and historic cottage at around 5:30 that evening.

I carried my bag up the painted steps of the white wrap-around porch and entered the heavy turquoise door. A blast of cold air conditioning and a grinning little woman greeted me. She was sitting behind an oversized desk in the corner of the gorgeous living room adorned with a white linen couch and palm plants.

"Hello! Welcome to The Shell House. Will you be checking in this evening?" She smiled like a Cheshire cat.

"I absolutely will," I said as she motioned for me to sit in a pastel wicker chair in front of her desk. "What a gorgeous place."

"Well, we're so glad you could stay with us. The home was

built in 1897 by Captain Delaney Whitten and his wife, Charlotte. Captain Whitten was…" She proceeded to delve into the history of the home, complete with hand gestures like Vanna introducing the next puzzle on *Wheel of Fortune.*

When I was sure I could answer all questions under the category of "THE SHELL HOUSE" on *Jeopardy!* , the petite brunette led me up a beautiful mahogany staircase to an antique door with recessed panels.

"What will you do on your stay?" she asked as she unlocked the door.

"I'm a writer," I said. "I came here for inspiration."

"Oh!" she exclaimed. "How lovely! As I'm sure you know, Ernest Hemingway wrote many of his well-known works in the second-story writing studio that adjoins his home on Whitehead Street, which is only a few blocks away."

"Oh, yes." I grinned. "My husband and I visited his home years ago. I'm anxious to go back. I'll be better prepared this time for all of the cats roaming around."

She opened the door to reveal a beautiful peach room with bamboo furniture and a bronze palm ceiling fan slowly and quietly slicing through the chilled air. "Here you are."

"This is perfect." I wheeled my luggage next to the bed and glanced out the floor-to-ceiling window that overlooked the upstairs porch and the tops of palm trees.

"Please let me know if you need anything during your stay, Mrs. Lambert. If you're hungry, our head chef, Alberto, will be hosting dinner at 6 on the lanai. On this evening's menu, we have stone crabs, corn on the cob and lime-kissed salad. Stone crabs are renowned for their sweet and succulent meat. The grilled…" The thorough tour guide began again, complete with smile and hand gestures.

When she was finished with the crustacean lesson, she left me alone to relax on the soft mint-colored comforter. I phoned Tim and the girls to check in, followed by a quick call to my sister. I didn't tell her I was in Key West to search for Leigh. Instead, I told her that I'd dropped the outlandish investigation and that Leigh's post card had, in fact, inspired me to change the setting of my novel and visit the port town for inspiration. Darcy encouraged me and said she was proud that I'd come to my senses.

I then called both Rusty and Grace. Grace told me she hadn't seen Baker and Joanna all day. I immediately feared they, too, had booked a flight to Key West in hopes to get to Leigh before I did.

Rusty had been listening to the recorder, but had heard nothing but silence and the quiet buzzing of Baker's refrigerator. He was eager to pose as the Rainbow salesman again and get the listening device's flash drive for Chief Haskins. He said he'd do that tomorrow if Joanna was home. I told him to keep me posted.

I went down to the poolside lanai at half past six and sat at a small round table covered with a white linen cloth and dim tea candle. Several tables surrounded the pool, but only three were occupied, including mine.

A young, kind Hispanic man in black pants and a crisp white shirt approached me with a smile and took my drink order. I asked for a glass of the house wine and a coffee. I knew a place as classy as this didn't serve my Whole Foods Red or Folgers. I would get stuck with a $20 glass of crushed grapes and a $12 cup of high-end Colombian brew, but I'd have to suck it up and make the best of it.

I looked around the patio and took in the massive palm trees and overflowing colorful landscape shadowed by the pink and orange dusky sky. Grace would certainly love to admire all of the foliage here.

An older couple sat together at the first table. The tea candle in the centerpiece illuminated the lady's yellow bouffant bun, brown skin tone and the sparkling chain dangling from the temple of her stylish glasses. She smiled at the man sitting across from her, who bore an uncanny resemblance to a sunbaked George Hamilton. They laughed over their meal and sipped their fruity concoctions.

The other table was also occupied by a couple in their mid-sixties. However, they weren't as stylish as George Hamilton and his bride. The woman at table two looked homely and pale, with blue-rinsed curls and an outdated floral blouse. I was unsure if her beau was sighted because, bless his heart, he was wearing two different patterns of plaid– on both his shirt and shorts.

Feeling like the fifth wheel to the old couples sharing the same concrete poolside as me, I pulled my phone from my purse and looked through Leigh's social media profile for the tenth time that day. I wanted to engrave her photos in my mind so I wouldn't miss her if I were to pass her on the street.

The waiter brought my expensive beverages, followed by a heavy cream-colored plate of steaming pink crab. I ate most of my meal alone, but when the stylish older couple was done with their food, they walked over to my table.

They introduced themselves as Verna and, ironically, George. They lived in Miami, but said they drove down to the Keys and stayed at The Shell House for a few days every other week. We exchanged basic information, and I invited them to sit at my table, but George declined, claiming the rum had run right through him and he needed to retire to their room. However, his bubbly, tanned lady accepted my offer and pulled out the white iron chair across from me.

"You see those two over there?" She hiccupped and nodded to the other older couple at table 2.

"Yes, ma'am." I took the last bite of my lime-kissed salad and pushed my plate away.

"They come down here every month or two to see their son. He's a fisherman. I think. They're from Minnesota or some cold, God-forsaken place like that. That's why they are so pale, see? Like sheets, aren't they? And that poor Pete didn't get the memo that plaid doesn't match plaid," she said as she winked at me and finished off her fuchsia drink. "Jorge! I'll take another!" She lifted her glass in the air.

"They don't even indulge. You ever heard of such a thing? To come all the way down here from Michigan and not even have a Key Lime Martini? Ludicrous." She hiccupped again.

I chuckled at the old, inebriated woman, with her navy blue nautical blouse and bright red lipstick stains on her teeth.

"So, tell me...I'm sorry. Tessa, was it?"

"Yes ma'am. Tessa," I confirmed.

"So, tell me, Tessa. What are you doing down here all alone? I see that sparkling rock on your finger. Where's your husband, if I can be frank?"

"He's back home in Mississippi with our children. I'm a writer. I came down here to hopefully cure my writer's block."

"Oh, wonderful!" Verna clapped her ring-covered hands together. "What are you writing? Do tell!"

"Well, it's the story of a young woman who falls in love with a thug from Monaco and ends up facing murder charges." I sipped the costly wine.

"Oh steamy." She leaned her elbows onto the table and hiccupped again. "And it takes place here? In Key West?"

"I think it will," I replied. "The French Riviera was the original setting, but it's hard for me to write about a place I've never been. Now I'm just trying to piece it all together and figure out what in the world a Monegasque thug is doing in Florida."

"Oh, honey, you'd be surprised. It's a melting pot down here. Beautiful thing, really. You're liable to hear five different languages while walking only a block. French is bound to be one of them."

"Well, I hope so. I'm eager to get out and explore the city tomorrow." I ran my finger across the rim of my wine glass.

"George and I are sailing on his brother's boat tomorrow, or I would be glad to show you around. I know everything about this glorious town. And Lord knows I'd rather spend the day with you. I've only known you ten minutes, but you sure seem like better company than my wretched sister-in-law. All she talks about is her lactose intolerance and bunions. I've been hearing about it for 42 years."

I laughed as the imaginary light bulb flickered to life above my sweaty, humid pony tail.

"Actually, Mrs. Verna, I was hoping to find an old friend of mine while I'm down here. She's been living here for a few months, but I haven't been able to get in touch with her. Maybe you know her?" I rummaged through my purse for my phone.

"I know everyone here, darling." She took the fruity drink from the waiter, Jorge, and gave him a flirtatious wink. "I met Hemingway when I was ten. He gave me a kitten."

I pulled up Leigh's social networking page and clicked on her profile photo.

"This is my friend. Have you seen her?" I handed the telephone to Verna.

She positioned her ruby glasses squarely over her eyes and studied the photo.

"Oh, my. You're in luck, dear. Yes, I've seen this young lady." She nodded.

"What?" I exclaimed. "Are you sure?"

"I remember that short haircut. She has such a pretty face. It's a shame it isn't framed by long hair. Tsk. Tsk." She shook her head. "I haven't spoken to her, but I've seen her several times down at Sloppy Joe's during lunch."

"You're sure? You've seen her?"

"I'm sure of it." She bobbed her head drunkenly and handed me the phone. "I never forget a face, except my own. Sometimes I look in the mirror and can't believe it's me. I forget this is what I look like now. I was 18 just yesterday." She gulped more of her drink.

"You don't know where she's staying?" I studied Leigh's photo.

"Going to bed so soon?" Verna called to the old northern couple as they passed by us.

"Yes, Verna," the pale lady snapped and quickly walked on, followed by her plaid husband.

"Sticks in mud, those two." Verna leaned back in her chair and fiddled with her anchor earring.

"You don't know where she's staying?" I asked again.

"No, I don't, dear, but each time I've seen her it's been at Sloppy Joe's Bar down on Duval. We usually go on Friday at lunch for crab cakes before we head back to Miami. She's been in there the last few times we've gone. I never forget a face."

"Well, this is excellent news," I said before drinking the rest of my wine with one swallow.

When Verna was too intoxicated to form complete sentences, I helped her up the shiny mahogany stairs as she hiccupped and sang a compilation of Barry Manilow tunes. When we reached her room just down the hall from mine, George, wearing black bikini underwear, a tight white t-shirt and heavy gold chain (and not the least bit embarrassed by it), thanked me for returning his beautiful bride in one piece.

My eyes still burning from the sight of the old fellow's hairy legs protruding from underwear smaller than mine, I immediately called Grace to tell her every detail of my evening. She absorbed all of the information I'd given her and then she said, "Tell me more about this George fellow. What was he wearing again?"

I also phoned Tim and the girls. I told them all about my lovely room at the bed and breakfast and how entertaining the elderly drunk lady was. I talked excitedly about Key West serving as the perfect setting for Penelope Broussard, and how I was eager to do some sightseeing. They had no idea I was going to search for the dead neighbor tomorrow.

SIXTEEN

The next morning, I woke bright and early to the smell of stout coffee and sizzling bacon wafting up the mahogany stairs. I hopped out of bed, fervent to hit the town and save my dead neighbor's life.

After I showered and dressed in a white tank top and khaki shorts, I went downstairs to see the old, pasty couple sitting alone at the bulky pastel dining table. They were quietly peering out the French doors that overlooked the lanai surrounded by greenery, sipping orange juice and picking at their bran muffins. I grinned at them and the lady with the tight blue perm returned a weak smile.

I grabbed a plate from the buffet table and filled it with melon, bacon and mini blueberry muffins. I didn't want to sit with the boring seniors, so I went onto the patio and took a seat at the same small table where I'd eaten supper the night before. I didn't see Verna or George. I assumed they were both sleeping off their rum hangovers.

When my plate was clean and I'd chugged 2 cups of the dark, expensive coffee, the petite tour guide approached me. She sat at the small iron table with me and asked about last night's meal, how I slept and my plans for the day. When I told her I was going to see the town, she suggested I rent a bicycle. Luckily she was in possession of a powder blue Huffy Beach Cruiser that had been acquired from the estate sale of a famous local captain. After listening to the history lesson on the vintage cycle, I was nervous to ride it. It would be just my luck to wreck the thing while dodging a cat and rip the significant wire basket off the front, but I accepted anyway.

I pedaled away from the B&B to the faint sound of construction on the island, my bulky straw purse resting in the basket and my hair blowing in the salty breeze. My flip flops pushed the pedals down narrow alleys littered with coconut husks and main streets bustling with speeding cabs. Sloppy Joe's wouldn't be open for a few hours, so I had some time to kill. I knew where I was going first.

When I reached Whitehead Street, I stopped the bike in front of Hemmingway's home. I breathed in the elegant Spanish colonial architecture with its green shutters and lush landscape. I could imagine

Penelope Broussard here, stealing a kiss from a Monegasque- (no, Cuban! Yes, Cuban) - gangster, before she was aware of what a ruthless man he really was and the trouble he was going to cause for her.

I hopped off the bicycle and walked it through the front gate and to the booth where a cordial lady greeted me. She told me I could park the bicycle next to her station, and I paid her for a tour. Already cats weaved between my legs and then disappeared into thick ferns and elephant ears in the emerald garden surrounding the home.

I walked onto the front porch and was welcomed by an eccentric tour guide with spikey gelled hair and an iguana on his shoulder.

"I'll be giving the first tour of the day in about 15 minutes." He smiled widely. "Or you are free to walk around at your own leisure!"

"I've been on the tour before," I replied, trying not to make eye contact with the massive lizard staring at me. "I just want to walk around this time if that's okay? I'm a writer. I'm here for inspiration."

"Oh, how wonderful!" He clapped his hairy hands donning black nail polish. "Be sure to check out Mr. Hemmingway's writing studio in the back. That ought to get your creative juices flowing!"

The way he slowly enunciated "creative juices" made me stifle the acid reflux that threatened to escape my lips.

"Thanks." I walked into the house.

Only a handful of people were in the home this early, so I had enough quiet to really absorb my surroundings. I flipped my flops along the creaking floors and examined the movie posters on the hallway wall. I took time to read each word of the framed letters written by the man himself. I peered into a bulky bookcase and reveled at the tattered copy of *The Old Man and the Sea*. I studied photos of Mr. Hemmingway holding up large fish somewhere on a boat in the middle of the Gulf of Mexico and admired wooden ships in glass cases. I scanned the photo of his white six-toed cat and read that sailors believed six-toed cats were good luck and wanted them aboard their ships, hence the plethora of odd-footed felines in this port town.

When I walked out the back door, I was greeted by the sound of faint meows over the rustling of palm leaves. Paw prints were stamped into the cement walkways that lead to the writing studio.

I climbed the black, iron staircase to Hemmingway's workspace. It was once connected to a catwalk that spanned across the gallery roof and connected to the master bedroom porch. How cool, I thought, to have an actual writing area instead of a small space at the kitchen counter.

I peered through the gate at the top of the stairs and into the room where Hemmingway wrote some of his notable works. A small round table sat in the middle of the room, topped with a vintage typewriter much like one I kept on a bookshelf in our living room. A calico cat sat next to the table, licking her paws, unaware of what a significant place she'd decided to take a bath. Another cat, bright orange, rested in front of a box fan in the corner that circulated the warm, humid air around the room.

I gawked into the space for nearly ten minutes, alone and quiet, absorbing all that I possibly could. Every book on the shelves, every animal mounted on the wall, every vase, every clock, the elegant chandelier, I studied it all. I let the inspiration seep into parts of my writing soul that had been void of all creativity for so long. I saw her here, Penelope Broussard. I saw her here, in Key West, touring this home with the troublemaking love of her life.

I left the property, rejuvenated, with a cell phone of photos for future reference. While walking the bicycle down Whitehead Street, I was struck with the overwhelming desire to find a pen and paper at that very moment and start scribbling the dialogue between Penelope and her boyfriend as they fled down alleys from the Key West police after being pinned for their crimes. However, that would have to wait. I knew another crime was going to take place if I didn't find Leigh Kilpatrick. It was almost noon, so I hoped I would find her at the bar.

I hopped back onto the bike and pedaled away from Hemmingway's. I made a right turn on a street with azalea petals spilling over the sidewalks and took a snapshot of the colorful buoy at the southernmost point of the continental United States. I sent it in a text to Tim and the girls, and Jules immediately replied, "Cool!"

Riding the Huffy alongside the aqua blue water, I dodged coconut hulls and watched a fancy yacht leave the port. I continued to take sightseeing photos for my family, as if I wanted to prove that this trip had nothing to do with Leigh Kilpatrick.

Sweat had begun to break on my brow when I reached the saloon on the corner of Duval and Greene. It was white brick, with SLOPPY JOE'S BAR painted in large red letters on both the front and the side of the building. Tim and I had stopped here on our whimsical trip a decade before. I vaguely remembered having one too many banana daiquiris and attempting to sing a Cher song in Spanish during karaoke hour.

I leaned the bike against the front of the building and said a prayer over it that no one would steal this piece of two-wheeled Key West history. Then I peered through one of the three opened front doors. The place was all but empty, as wait staff hurried around and set tables for the upcoming lunch crowd. But there, at the bar, was a woman with a tousled grown-out pixie cut and bronze skin. She leaned over a tall straw and nursed a Bushwhacker. Then she popped a French fry in her mouth and watched the television screen above a row of liquor bottles behind the bar. It was Leigh Kilpatrick, alive and in the flesh.

My heart began to pound in my chest, much harder than it had when I struggled to pedal the heavy bicycle up a steep hill earlier that morning. It pounded so loudly that I could hear it radiating from inside my body. My palms began to produce an unusual amount of sweat and my mouth became dry as cotton. I concluded that I'd never been more nervous in my life, including the time I read a terribly cheesy poem that I'd written about "the real world" at my high school graduation ceremony.

Before I backed out and said forget this— let Leigh Kilpatrick get what's coming to her— I mustered up a huge dose of courage, cleared my throat and shuffled my woven flip flops towards her. I silently stood only a few feet away from Leigh until she finally looked up to me. Her eyes grew as big as saucers and her mouth dropped open so wide that I was certain her chin was going to hit the bulky bar covered in nicks and scratches.

"Hi, Leigh," I managed to croak.

She said nothing and continued to gawk at me in disbelief.

"I tracked you down to see about getting my Tupperware back." An awkward chuckle escaped my lips.

Leigh continued to soundlessly eye me, her mouth still parted, when my phone rang. I frantically rummaged through the straw purse to find it and see my mother's name on the caller ID. Of course it was my mother. She only called when I was in the middle of something important.

Like greeting the dead neighbor.

.

LEIGH

When my grandmother was utterly surprised by something, she'd declare, "As I live and breathe!" I don't think I've ever muttered that phrase in my life– although I've been shocked countless times– but when I looked up from the French fries and Bushwhacker setting before me at Sloppy Joe's Bar in Key West, Florida, to see my neighbor from Pontotoc Springs, Mississippi, I shouted the words in my mind.

Tessa Lambert. Perfect, blonde, physically fit, annoying little Tessa Lambert was standing before me, 1100 miles from her home. Tessa Lambert with her silky ponytail and flawless skin and normal suburban life was standing right here. Tessa Lambert with her handsome, broad-chested husband who had a thick head of dark hair and wore loafers every day. Tessa Lambert with her pretty little girls who answered to southern belle family names and had bouncing locks and a fluffy puppy chasing them on perfectly manicured Bermuda grass. Tessa Lambert who placed a store-bought German chocolate cake in Tupperware and tried to pass it off to me as homemade. Yes, that Tessa Lambert was standing right in front of me with Ray Bans covering her eyes and a huge straw purse that concealed half of her upper body hanging over her tanned shoulder.

The sound of my grandmother's voice was incessantly floating through my head, but I managed to hear perfect little Tessa Lambert mumble something about Tupperware and then she pulled a ringing phone from the huge purse. She grimaced at the name on the caller ID and turned off the ringer. Then she removed the aviator sunglasses from her eyes, used them as a headband to keep blonde strands of hair out of her face, and she focused again on me.

"So, how's it going?" She sat on the barstool next to me, as if we were old friends meeting for a drink after work.

Still words failed me.

"I can see all over your face how shocked you are to see me, Leigh." She hung the purse over the back of the stool. "I can't say I blame you. I mean, you're supposed to be *dead*."

She whispered the word and made quotation marks with her fingers, but still I couldn't speak.

"Look," she said as she cleared her throat, "I don't want you to freak out. You look like you're about to freak out. I'm not here to blow your cover or anything, but I know why you're here. I know you're waiting on Baker. I know about Mack."

Mack? She knew about Mack. How did perfect little Tessa Lambert know anything about a ruthless drug dealer who'd gladly slit someone's throat without thinking twice about it? Had he recruited her? Threatened her? Had he forced her to come here and demand the money I owed him?

"I don't judge you for any of that, Leigh," she spoke quietly so no one but I could hear her. "I don't care that you faked your own death. I don't care why you're here. I know about all of that, but I don't care. What I do care about is what's going to happen to you if you stay here."

I wanted to speak. I really wanted to speak. I've never been speechless. I've never been the type of person to sit silently while I listened to some perfect little suburbanite wearing head to toe Gap apparel sputter and drone. But as I examined her sitting before me on the barstool, the words just wouldn't come.

"Baker isn't coming, Leigh."

She rummaged through the straw bag and pulled out several photographs, then handed them to me. I saw my handsome Baker and some red-headed child sitting in the auburn Adirondack chairs on our back porch in Mississippi. My heart began to palpitate as I looked at the infidelity in living color– the love of my life and another woman.

"I'm sorry," she added.

I looked up from the photos and into her chocolaty eyes. Tessa Lambert. She was the girl who caught all the breaks. I was annoyed just looking at her because she was the very type of girl who'd always made my life hell. She was the epitome of all that I hated. She was the one who stole my boyfriends. She was the one who crushed my self-esteem. She was the one I got high to forget.

She probably sang the cheers of her youth at her daughter's

basketball games. She wasn't blackballed from the Chi O-something's because she had a dysfunctional family. She didn't have to prostitute herself to get through nursing school. The only thing Tessa Lambert ever worried about was what color ribbon to tie around her ponytail.

Stupid Tessa Lambert with her perfect life. She probably had a handsome, rich daddy with a corner office overlooking some big, bustling city. Her mother had perfected a strawberry cake recipe and would be devastated to know her little girl took the new neighbors a store-bought German chocolate. Stupid Tessa Lambert with her upper-class upbringing had no idea what it was like to have an absent father and a mother who cared more about herself than her children. She didn't know what it was like to be stuck, to long, to mourn. Perfect little Tessa Lambert didn't have a clue what it was like to be me. And here she was, undoubtedly ecstatic to reveal the news of my husband's infidelity. She loved saying the words and spilling the secrets that would be the end of me. Girls like her loved to crush girls like me. Marybeth Martin. Tracy Shelley. Eliza Studstill. Tessa Lambert.

"Get out of here." My voice finally worked.

A surprised look covered her smooth complexion for a moment, and then she sighed.

"I'll have what she's having." She looked past me to the bartender and then bobbed her head at the melting Bushwhacker in front of me. "I don't usually indulge this early in the day, but I could use a drink right about now and that looks delicious. It's got Kahlua and what?"

"Black rum," I replied dryly.

"Look, let me just finish explaining and then I'll gladly get out of here, okay?" She shrugged. "You remember Grace? Grace McKinney?"

"The old broad with the cat that always crapped on my lawn? Yes."

"Well, Grace and I were suspicious of Baker when you *died*." Again she whispered the word and made quotations with her fingers. "He was entirely too happy for a bereaved husband. He was dancing around the driveway, drinking, celebrating even. He put a for sale sign on your car. He was jovially throwing Hamburger Helper into his cart at Piggly Wiggly only days after you were *buried*. It just didn't add up."

I felt a twinge in my chest at her words, a twinge of sorrow that he didn't even appear to be sad when I was gone.

"And then he really blew it when he had this chick move in." She pointed at the photos on my lap. "The dirt wasn't even settled on your supposed grave yet, and here she was, moving right in. I know it's hard for you to hear, Leigh, but they were making out on the front porch for the whole cove to see."

I didn't want to hear this. I didn't want to become emotional at her words. I didn't want Tessa Lambert to see me cry.

"Even Dr. Parker seemed more upset about your death than Baker. Mr. Anderson played Elvis' *He Touched Me* album on repeat for a few days when he heard the news. It was so sad, you know? Our young, beautiful neighbor ending her life like that. We were all confused by it, upset about it and we didn't even know you," she said and shrugged sympathetically. "So, with a little investigative work, Grace and Rusty— oh, you know Rusty!"

"Who is Rusty?" I snapped.

"You dated his brother Ralphie. Do you remember Ralphie Ballard?"

"Ralphie Ballard? The vacuum cleaner guy with the comic book obsession?" I vaguely remembered the meaningless relationship.

"Yeah, Ralphie went to your funeral. That's a pretty nice thing for a guy to do after his girlfriend tried to set him on fire for ordering pineapple on her pizza, you think?" She winked.

How did stupid Tessa Lambert know about the pineapple pizza fiasco? I was still confused as to why this twit was even here.

"Well, I write with Ralphie's brother, Rusty. Rusty, Grace and I were all suspicious of Baker. Originally we though he killed you. I mean, he seemed glad you were gone, and I watch enough Hitchcock movies to know that made him the prime suspect. So, we planted a bug in your house. We can call and listen in on it right now if you'd like. It's still there," she insisted.

I shook my head and sat the photos next to my cold French fries. "You did what?"

"I know it all sounds crazy, absolutely absurd, but that's why I'm here. I heard him, Leigh. I heard him telling the new girl, Joanna, everything. They were sitting at the kitchen table and he told her you faked your death. He said you were down here waiting on him. And," she hesitated, "he said he wasn't coming to be with you. I'm sorry, Leigh, but he says he loves her. He isn't coming."

My head began to spin the way it did when I was coming down from a three day bender. I steadied my palms on the bar and squeezed my eyes closed.

"You're lying," I spoke to interrupt the echo of her callous words ringing in my ears.

"I'm not lying, and I'm not here to break your heart. I'm here to warn you. You've got to get out of this place," she begged.

"Warn me of what?"

"He says he knows people down here. He said you're a loose end. Something bad is going to happen to you, Leigh. It's going to happen soon. You've got to get out of here."

"You're lying!" I said again.

"Do you really think I've come all the way down here to lie to you? I'm only here to tell you this because I couldn't live with myself if I knew this information and then something really happened to you."

Had I gotten high this morning? Was this all a dream? Was this a hallucination? I'd had plenty of hallucinations. I'd seen Ronald Reagan, purple snow, Care Bears. Was this a hallucination, too, or was Tessa Lambert of Sugar Creek Cove in Pontotoc Springs, Mississippi really here warning me that my husband was going to kill me? Was she trying to trick me? Was this real?

"We can call the recorder right now. You can call in and listen to your home right now, Leigh. You'll hear Joanna. You'll hear her watching *Maury* or some other ignorant television show. She's in that house, with Baker and her little brothers, and she has no plans of leaving. Baker has no plans of leaving, either. I'm not lying to you. We can call—"

"Just shut up a minute. Just shut up!" I shouted, leaned forward and sucked the rum through the straw. "I have to think."

Tessa Lambert did shut up. She received her drink identical to mine and sipped on it, as the bamboo ceiling fans above us circulated warm air. A group of loud, laughing customers entered. The expensive cameras hanging from their necks and the Conch Republic or Mile Marker 0 t-shirts they all wore gave them away as sightseers. An older man in a Hawaiian shirt and straw hat walked onto the bar's stage, sat on a stool and began tuning his acoustic guitar for the lunch set.

I looked back to the photographs on my lap. I didn't know the young girl in the photos, but I assumed she was the reason he'd taken so many trips down to Gulfport. He said he had a client down there with a sick horse that he was determined to help, but he never answered my calls when he was gone. I knew something didn't add up, but who was I to question Baker Kilpatrick and get a swift kick from that size 13?

Maybe perfect little Tessa Lambert was telling the truth. Maybe she was the first of her breed to actually look out for me and show me kindness.

And maybe Baker wasn't coming. It was true that he hadn't contacted me once since I'd been in Key West. Maybe he was happier without me. Maybe he didn't want to be around all these cats after watching that old lady's crap in our yard all the time. Maybe he really was going to have some thug down here break my neck and throw me into the ocean. Maybe I wasn't even surprised by it.

"Yakutsk," I mumbled.

"Bless you," Tessa replied.

"No." I shook my head at her stupidity. "It's cold there. It's too cold for cats. It's too cold for Baker. He'll never find me there."

"Leigh," she said as she reached over and touched my arm and I jerked it away, "I'm sorry."

In that moment, I no longer loathed stupid Tessa Lambert. I still found her annoying and envied the perfect life she'd always lived, but suddenly I felt like she really was an old friend meeting me after work for drinks. She was meeting me for drinks to tell me that my estranged husband was going to have me killed.

"I have to ask this. I'm sorry, and you may not even tell me, but I can't leave here without asking." She flinched uneasy on her stool. "We saw a body being wheeled out of your home that morning. You had a funeral. Someone is buried in a plot at Magnolia Hill Cemetery. I know there was a genuine death certificate. I have to ask. Who was it? Who died?"

I looked away from Tessa Lambert's inquiring eyes and watched the palm trees blowing on the other side of the open doors. A storm was coming. I could smell it in the air.

"I heard Baker confess everything to Joanna. I heard him say he gave someone pills, but I didn't hear the name. Who was it, Leigh?" She continued to badger.

I hadn't felt remorse for it. Not once. But as Tessa Lambert begged me for a name, I felt an aching pang. For the first time since Baker and I had planned to do this, to kill her and make people believe she was me, I felt guilty. And I only felt guilty because she'd been killed in vain. If Baker wasn't coming, if he wasn't upholding his end of the deal, then my sister had been killed in vain.

SEVENTEEN

She wanted to tell me. Leigh Kilpatrick wanted to clear her conscious, get it off her chest, confess the name. It was evident as she chewed on her lip and shifted her eyes around the bar, now bustling with tourists eager to try the establishment's famous ground beef and tomato sauce sandwich.

"What are you going to do?" she finally asked. "Are you going to have us arrested? Is that what you want? Send Baker and me both to prison for murder?"

"No." I shook my head. "Would I come all the way down here to warn you about Baker's plans if I wanted to have you arrested?"

"What about Baker? You're going to tell the police everything you know? You're going to tell them he killed someone and reported that it was me? You're going to tell them he wants me, the real me, dead now?"

"Is that what you want me to do?" I asked.

She thought long and hard for a few moments and then adamantly nodded her head.

"Absolutely," she said with certainty. "If he's not going to live up to his end of the deal, if he's not going to spend the rest of his life with me, then he isn't going to spend it with this floozy." She thumped Joanna's face on the photograph in her lap. "He can rot in jail for the rest of his life."

"I won't mention any of this, Leigh. This…being here, talking to you— this involves me, and I don't want to be involved. My husband doesn't even know the real reason I'm here. I don't need this in my life. My crackpot mother is enough trouble for me." I shook my head as Leigh's eyes caught mine. "I absolutely won't say anything about being here or talking to you. I'm going to put together an anonymous package and include those photos and the flash drive with the recording of Baker's confession. I'm going to send all of that to the police. I'm going to be stealthy about all of it— wear gloves, mail it from some podunk post office in Itawamba County. They'll never lift a fingerprint or link the package to Grace, Rusty or me. They'll assume

Baker first killed someone in your home and then had you killed down here, and you'll be scot-free to live in whatever cold climate you desire," I stated with certainty.

"You've thought his through, haven't you?" she asked.

"I'm a writer," I said as I shrugged. "My mind is constantly running through scenarios, plots, plans. I also watch a lot of Hitchcock and made-for-TV movies. I had no problem thinking this through."

Leigh Kilpatrick chuckled. She actually chuckled, only for a split second, and she no longer looked at me like I was the bane of her existence.

"Look, I kind of get it. I mean, I've seen enough episodes of *Snapped* to know what's happened here. You were trying to do a noble, good thing and get away from that junkie life. Baker brainwashed you into killing someone to save yourself. Of course you'd do what he asked. You loved him. You still do. I see that love in your eyes, Leigh. I saw how crushed you were when I told you he wasn't coming here to be with you. Your love for him, infatuation with him, is why you did what you did.

"And I can see the remorse on your face. I see it, Leigh. I'm not interested in turning you in to the police or involving myself any further in this. I just need to know. I need to know who it was. I need this to end. I need the last piece to this puzzle so I can sleep at night. So I can finish my novel. So I can enjoy the rest of my summer. So I can move on with my life. Maybe if you tell me, confess it to me, you can move on with yours?"

Chatter filled the airy bar and the corner of the napkins under our drinks flapped in the wind. The guitarist tuned then strummed, tuned then strummed. Leigh finally leaned in close to me, her eyes still examining the photos that I'd taken on Grace's roof as a plastic spoon of organic peanut butter poked out of my mouth.

"My sister," she spoke in almost less than a whisper.

A knot formed in my throat, a knot the size of the coconut hulls that I'd dodged on the bike ride here.

"My stupid sister." She wiped her nose as tears welled up in her blue eyes. "It was my sister."

"Your twin," I said and swallowed the lump.

"Laurel," she whispered. "She's dead. She died in vain. He's not coming and she died in vain. Nothing. My sister died for nothing."

Words wouldn't form. I had no idea what to say, how to react, if I should try to console this obviously unstable woman sitting next to me. I've never had anyone confess to me that they murdered anyone, much less their twin. It was too much for this boring suburbanite to comprehend.

"Mack was relentless. He was harassing me for money every single day. He was showing up at the hospital and Baker's clinic. He said he'd kill us both if we didn't pay him. We didn't know what to do and he wouldn't leave us alone, and then that stupid Eliza Studstill caught me stealing pills. I was going to lose my job and be arrested," she confessed as the tears dripped down her nose. "Baker knocked me around, but I deserved it. He tried to keep me on the straight and narrow, spare the rod and spoil the child, you know? But we didn't know how to get out of this. This was just too much for us to bear. And then it came to us! I couldn't go to jail, and it was so obvious that we had to make Mack believe I was dead. And it was obvious that it should be my sister. It was perfect. What a pathetic life she was living anyway. She was strung out and living in Section 8 housing down in Mobile. She was such a disappointment to the entire family. She had two babies and gave them away. She'd ruined their lives, dodging in and out at her convenience, leaving them without a stable mother. She ruined my life, too. She was the one who got me hooked on drugs. She was the one who suggested we get stoned to forget what our parents had done to us, to forget the people who wronged us. I hated her for that, for enabling me for so many years. I hated her for getting me hooked on that crap. Baker said killing her was the right thing to do." She wiped her soaking eyes with the back of her hand.

"I found her on Facebook. Can you believe it? A junkie, with no home or car or assets, but she had a Facebook account? We hadn't spoken in years, but I messaged her to make amends and invited her to visit. I told her we'd get high all weekend. She'd have a warm shower and a clean bed. I wired her bus fare and she was in Mississippi in two days." She let it all spill out, the tears continuing to fall. "I gave her a makeover. *Wouldn't it be great to look like twins again, Laurel?* I cut and dyed her hair myself. We were identical again. And I was looking at her in the bathroom mirror and realized she still looked better than me, despite all of the drugs we'd both done. She always was the prettier one.

"I fixed her Vodka and then more of it. One bottle gone, half of the second until she was lying across the ottoman passed out drunk. And Baker…Baker started feeding her pills. She was so out of it that she didn't know what he was doing. Ambien, Xanax, Hydrocodone, you name it. I had prescriptions for all of those things. He was crushing them and pouring them down her throat. She was choking, and he just kept giving them to her until she went limp. Pill bottles were empty, liquor bottles were empty, gone," she cried, "and then my sister was gone, too."

I didn't realize that I was also crying until a tear raced down my cheek and fell onto my shorts. I quickly smudged the wet trail away as Leigh continued to speak, pouring out her confession as if it were the most cathartic thing she'd ever done. As if it were something she'd longed to do.

"I couldn't watch it. I went upstairs. I didn't cry. I didn't feel guilty, but I couldn't watch the life drain out of her like that. But then I was glad about it, you know? She was finally at peace. No more addiction or arrests or problems for Laurel. She didn't have to feel guilty anymore. Our family didn't have to bail her out anymore. It was done, and it was the right thing to do. She died to save me. It was the right thing to do. I really thought it was.

"We drug her into the kitchen and staged everything. We put the empty bottles on the floor next to her, and I wrote a letter and left it on the counter. In the suicide note, I said I couldn't face the embarrassment of being fired and charged with stealing pills from the hospital pharmacy. Then I looked at her there on the floor, my twin, pale and covered in vomit, and it was such an eye-opener. I knew if I didn't get clean, if I didn't get away from Mack and that life, then I would end up just like her. It was like looking at my own death.

"I told him I wanted an extravagant funeral. Baker would pay for it all on credit, but it didn't matter because he was going to disappear and come to Key West to be with me anyway. They'd never find him. The pearl white casket would be closed. Baker would insist. My aunt Carla wouldn't see the body and know it was Laurel instead of me. She was the only one who could really tell us apart. Our own mother mixed up our names half the time. It was going to work, he said. Baker is so smart, and he said it was a foolproof plan. No one was going to check fingerprints or DNA to make sure it was me. We were identical. If it walks like a duck, you know?

"When everything was staged and my sister was dead on the kitchen floor, Baker drove me to Little Rock. I used her ID to buy a ticket and catch a bus that morning. I was in Key West the next night. He went home and called the police. Told them he woke up to find me dead in the kitchen with a suicide note. My sister is gone now and for what? He didn't hold up his end of the deal. She died for nothing. She died for nothing."

"Oh, Leigh." We both wiped our wet faces as the guitarist opened his set with "Cheeseburger in Paradise". "You have—"

"Press charges, Tessa." Her sad face suddenly hardened with anger. "You send that son of a bitch to jail. Do what you have to do."

She pulled a wad of cash from the pocket of her denim shorts and threw it next to the half-empty Bushwhacker glass.

"What are you doing?" I studied her, unsure what to do. Should I just let her pay for her French fries and go? Should I try to stop this unbalanced woman who had idly stood by while her own sister was poisoned?

"I'm getting the out of here. Damn this heat. Damn these cats. Damn Jimmy Buffet." She grabbed her pink clutch from the bar and hurried toward the exit. She halted before she stepped her wedged sandal into the sun, and she turned to look at me.

"Thanks, Tessa," she mouthed as she held up her hand and produced a weak grin.

Then she was gone.

EIGHTEEN

Soon after Leigh left the beach bar, I dialed both Rusty and Grace. I told them the details of my shocking conversation with her, as they sat silently stunned on the other end of the line. Rusty reported that he still hadn't heard any conversation in Baker's home, and Grace confirmed that his BMW and Joanna's Honda were both missing from their driveway. This made me incredibly nervous that they were in the Florida Keys with me, possibly going to spot me pedaling the blue cycle through town and attempt to have me thrown into the ocean as shark bait with Leigh.

They both convinced me to come home as soon as possible. After booking a flight for 2:15 PM the following afternoon, I called Tim to let him know that I'd gotten what I'd come for and when to expect me.

I spent the rest of the day touring the island on the beach bike, as thunder bellowed from the dark clouds, but rain never poured. When the sky cleared, I lounged on the sand in a rented chair with a mojito in my hand. I also anxiously watched over my shoulder for Baker and Joanna or a hired ruffian wielding a switchblade.

While lolling on the beach and watching waves lap onto the rocky shore, Leigh continued to weigh heavily on my mind. I couldn't imagine what kind of traumatic and dysfunctional life she'd lived to even contemplate killing her twin sister, much less agreeing to actually go through with it. I didn't know if I was doing the right thing by allowing her to go free, but I sincerely hoped she'd find a fresh start and a glimmer of happiness in the cold climate that she sought.

I slurped the rest of the minty mojito, my Mississippi skin frying on the beach so close to the equator, and I pulled up Google maps on my phone. I wanted to research that far off place that Leigh had sneezed earlier.

Yakutsk is cold and clear across the map. I was the only one who knew where she was going. I didn't even divulge her new Russian address to Grace or Rusty, and I never would. Baker Kilpatrick, Mack, anyone who hoped to harm Leigh would never know where to find her, either, because I sure wasn't going to tell them.

That evening for dinner, I met George and Verna on the lanai for crab cakes. I enjoyed the conversation with the two snazzy sexagenarians, but my thoughts still drifted back to the meeting with Leigh. The story was so surreal each time I thought about it. I would never have imagined drugs, demise and death, both fake and real, would come to our country cul-de-sac.

"Did you have a good day, dear?" Verna asked as she sipped her Chardonnay and left ruby red lipstick on the rim of the wine glass.

"I did." I cleared my throat. "Going to Hemmingway's really helped my writer's block. I'm eager to get home and start working."

"Wonderful news," she said as she took a bite of the lump crab. "George, did I tell you that Tessa is a writer?"

"Oh, wow." He chewed his food and glanced at me over the dim flicker of the tea candle in the middle of the small, round table. "What do you write?"

"Well, I'm a freelance writer for several parenting magazines, but I came down here for inspiration to finish a mystery novel I've been working on for years. It's about a French girl who gets caught up in a scandal with this thug from Monaco, although after being here, I think he's going to be rewritten as Cuban."

"Doesn't that sound delightful, George? It sounds like something I'd read, doesn't it?" Verna squealed enthusiastically.

"It does," George said and then took a swig of his liquor. "Throw a half-naked man in a loin cloth on the cover and Vern will definitely buy a copy."

I grinned as the old lady with more makeup than Tammy Faye winked at me.

"It sounds like your day was better than mine," she said. "God bless my sister-in-law and her bunions. I heard about them for five hours on the open sea today. She's finally got an appointment with that new podiatrist, George. That man will need extensive therapy after seeing her feet. The good Lord knows I do."

"She needs to see an orthopedic and just have both of those

things amputated." George gave a robust belly laugh and pushed his empty plate away.

Verna hiccupped as I chuckled.

"What about your friend? The one with the pretty face and boyish hair? Did you find her in town today?" She guzzled the last shot of wine.

"I did." I wiped my mouth with my napkin. "We had a great time catching up. She's doing great down here. Really loves it."

"What's not to love?" Verna held up her hands. "I hate to go back to Miami in the morning. Are we coming back next week, George?"

"We've got that grand opening in Ft. Lauderdale." He pulled a cigar from the pocket of his coral-colored linen shirt. "But maybe we can swing it the week after."

"George and I own 23 tanning salons along the Atlantic coast," Verna clarified.

Does George tan at all 23 of them every day? I thought as I eyed the man's leathery skin.

"What about your parents, Tessa? What line of work are they in?" She held up her empty wine glass to summon a refill from the waiter.

"Well," I said before finishing the last bite of crab, "my father died when I was really young, and my mother and I aren't close. My grandparents raised my sister and me, but they passed away a few years back."

"Oh, dear." Her face softened. "I'm so sorry."

"It's okay. I've come to accept that my mother and I will never have a relationship."

"That's terrible, Tessa. As long as there's a breath left in your mother's body, you should strive for some kind of connection with her."

"You don't know my mother." I shook my head. "She went crazy when my father died. A switch flipped or something. I don't know. She practically gave my sister and me to our grandparents. She didn't want us anymore, and she still doesn't. She only calls us when she needs something."

"Tsk," Verna sighed. "That's tragic."

"I guess." I sipped my water.

"Tell her about your mother, Vern. Tell her what you went through," George said before exhaling cigar smoke.

"Oh, she doesn't want to hear all of that," Verna said as she tugged at her beaded fuchsia earring.

"Then I'll tell her." George flicked the cigar's ashes to the empty plate before him. "Vern's mother, Doreen, was a real pill. She wasn't much of a mama to Vern or any of her girls. She didn't give her children away to grandparents or anything like your mother did, but she didn't count for much, did she, Vern?"

Verna shook her head and sipped on the fresh glass of wine.

"She called Vern one day and asked her to come up to Orlando and visit, but Vern didn't want to go. I didn't blame her any, because Doreen wasn't good for much but telling Vern everything wrong she'd done with her life. So Vern didn't make the trip, but her sisters did. They went to Orlando that weekend and Doreen apologized for all of her wrongs. Vern's sisters said she was awfully remorseful about a whole lot of things, and you know what?"

"No? What?" I shook my head at the tanned man with sparkling, silver hair.

"She died the very next day. Doreen wasn't sick or anything. She just said she wanted her girls with her that weekend. Told them she had this nudge to make things right. She fell over dead from a heart attack the very next day." George sucked on the stout-smelling cigar.

"Oh, Mrs. Verna." I reached out and touched her wrinkled ring-covered hand.

"Now ask Verna what kind of regret she feels for not going up to Orlando that weekend. That's been, what, 17 or 18 years ago and she still hasn't gotten over it," he replied.

"No," she said. "I haven't. I should have gone when my mother called. She apologized to each one of my sisters for very specific things she'd done to them. I know she was going to try to make amends about significant things she'd done to me, too, but I didn't go. She tried to explain why she wanted me to come. She said she wanted to make some things right, but I just blew her off. That's the biggest regret of my life," she said. "Well, that and not auditioning for the Rockettes when I had the chance. I would have made a real fine Rockette."

"I'm so sorry," I said.

"The point of that story George has bored you with is this, Tessa. Make amends with your mama. She may not be the best one, but she's the only one you've got. You don't want to live with the guilt that I do. When she calls and needs something, you help her all you can. Who knows what may happen, what she may apologize for, what wrongs could be made right if you just give her the chance to make them."

I gazed into this old lush's eyes, glazed over from her fourth glass of wine, and thought maybe she was right. She licked lipstick from her teeth as I agreed that I would make more of an effort with my mother.

Verna and George shared more stories about their youth and their children. Verna kicked back another glass of wine, George finished his cigar and we traded phone numbers and addresses. We conversed as we walked the mahogany stairs to our neighboring rooms. I told them I hoped to meet them again, gave a wine-reeking Verna a hug and unlocked my door.

"Let me know when that spectacular novel is finished," she called to me from her doorway.

"Yes, ma'am, I certainly will," I promised.

"And make things right with your mother." She shook a wrinkled finger at me before closing her door. I smiled and went inside to pack my suitcase.

NINETEEN

I nearly died on the flight from Key West to Charlotte. No, not because of engine failure or a gas leak or a sizzling lightning strike that sent the aircraft plummeting into the ocean. No, I nearly died from shock when I saw Baker Kilpatrick frantically board the plane only moments before takeoff.

It was apparent that he was frazzled and out of breath from racing down the jet bridge. He was running late, and I was incredibly thankful for it. Otherwise we would have caught sight of each other in the small Key West airport while waiting to board. That certainly would've been the most awkward, and terrifying, moment of my life.

I slid down in my seat near the back of the Airbus. A perturbed-looking flight attendant watched Baker as he struggled to shove his duffel bag into the overhead compartment. When he was finally done cramming the bag into the small space, he gave her a cocky smile and sat in his seat at the front of the plane.

My heart pounded in my chest for the duration of the two-hour flight. I was certain I was going to keel over from a heart attack. It was too much stress for this Mississippi housewife. This entire Kilpatrick scandal had surely shaved a good 10 years off my life, and I didn't know how much more I could take.

I gnawed on peanuts and gulped water, staving off the urge to pee in my pink capris pants. I kept my head hung low; terrified that Baker was going to see me, flushed and perspiring and sticking out like a sore thumb in the aisle seat near the lavatory. I was terrified he was going to confront me, and I wouldn't be clever enough to come up with a plausible excuse as to why I was leaving Key West. I was terrified he was going to discover my involvement, pull out a gun and shoot me right there in my cramped seat as we sailed across the summer blue sky.

When the plane finally landed in North Carolina, I took my sweet time exiting. I pretended to lose my ear buds beneath the seat and insisted that everyone on the aisles behind me go ahead. When only the incredibly annoyed flight attendant and I remained on the plane, I pretended to give up on finding the imaginary ear buds, gathered my things and walked down the jet bridge. I shifted the weight of my carryon from one shoulder to another and begged the good Lord not to let Baker and I cross paths in the bustling airport. I prayed that we weren't booked for the same flight to Memphis, and if we were, that we weren't sitting close enough to one another to share peanuts.

I didn't see Baker among the sea of faces crowding the Charlotte airport. I boarded the people mover, keeping my head down and watching for him out of the corner of my eye. When I reached my terminal on the other side of the airport, I slumped down in a seat and hid behind a newspaper.

I called Rusty while on the layover to Memphis. I told him that I'd seen Baker on the flight, and he became exceedingly concerned and nervous for me. He said he still hadn't heard any conversation in the home, although I hadn't seen Joanna and the boys with Baker on the flight. We didn't know where they were.

I chewed my nails until the plane to Memphis was full and the doors were shut. I thoroughly examined every face on the aisles surrounding me and heaved a collective sigh of relief that Baker wasn't on board. As we taxied down the runway, I relaxed my tense body.

Although my posture eased, my mind was frantic. Had Baker seen me in Key West? Had he spared my life only to burn my house to the ground while I slept inside? Had he gotten to Leigh before she left for Russia? Had I even saved her? Any joy or satisfaction that I'd experienced because I thought I'd done a good, noble thing by warning her was now gone. Baker may have had her killed moments after she left Sloppy Joe's Bar. And I may be next.

When I arrived home at 7PM on Friday, safe and somewhat sound, I immediately noticed that neither Baker's BMW nor Joanna's Honda were in the Kilpatrick driveway. I pulled my Tahoe into the garage, grabbed my luggage and raced inside my empty home. Tim was working late, Jules was still at the water park with a friend and

Grace was watching Ellis. I let Oreo outside to pee and then crept through my silent house with a butcher knife in my hand. I looked under every piece of furniture and behind every shower curtain, petrified I would find Baker waiting for me and with a Saturday night special in his hand– a Saturday night special with a barrel that's blue and cold. Those ain't good for nothing but putting snooping housewives like me six feet in a hole.

When I concluded that no weapon-yielding lunatics were hiding in my home, I let the dog back inside and headed over to Grace's house to get Ellis. Before I could step over the garden of monkey grass surrounding her front porch, Baker's BMW sailed down the street and pulled into his driveway. I froze in my tracks as he got out of the car and walked to his door with the duffel bag over his shoulder. He looked up and noticed me standing awkwardly in Grace's flower bed, but it appeared that he didn't give me a second thought. He didn't call out to me or charge toward me or even look at me as if he knew where I'd been. He just nonchalantly glanced at me for a moment and then looked back to his keys in his hand before unlocking his door and going inside his home.

I exhaled the built-up tension and worry and nervousness. I stood there in the brown mulch, breathing out for at least 20 seconds, and Grace finally opened her front door.

"What are you doing, dear? I saw you through my dining room window just standing here with your mouth dropped open. Are you all right?"

"Woman, I'm peachy. I'm absolutely peachy." I smiled at her. "Where's my little girl?"

"Hey, Mama," Ellis called from the foyer before rushing onto the front porch to hold me. "Ms. Grace made her brownies without nuts just for me. She knows how much I hate nuts. Oh, and she used organic flour!"

"Delicious." I held her and kissed the top of her head. "Go get your things together. I need to get home and start supper."

"Did you bring me anything?" She looked up at me, her eyes twinkling with curiosity.

"Maybe," I said, winking at her. "Get your stuff and let's go home and find out."

She raced into the house and left Grace and me alone, the warm summer wind wafting over us and the ferns hanging from the porch.

"So everything is taken care of? Leigh is okay?" she asked quietly as we both looked at Baker's home. "Oh, I see his car is back."

"He was in Key West, Grace," I murmured. "He was with me on the flight to Charlotte. I don't know if Leigh is safe or not. I don't know if he found her."

"He was there? He was on your flight!" she exclaimed and touched my arm. "Did he see you, Tessa?"

"No." I chewed on my bottom lip. "I don't think so. When he pulled up a few minutes ago, he didn't look at me oddly or anything. I don't think he saw me in Key West, and if he found Leigh, I don't think she told him I was there. I think I'm okay."

"Oh, honey." She shook her head. "This is too much. I'm too old for this. When will it all be over?"

"I'm going to call the recorder when I get home to hear if he says anything about being down there, about finding Leigh. Rusty will go get the flash drive tomorrow, and I'll send it to the police. Then it'll be over, Grace." I abruptly quit speaking when Ellis bounded onto the porch with her purse, headphones and iPod.

"See you girls later." Grace patted Ellis on the shoulder. "Keep me posted, Tessa."

I nodded and Ellis thanked Grace for the nut-free brownies. We walked across the grass as Grace went inside and shut the door.

I gave Ellis a small glass dolphin, t-shirt and children's mystery book that I'd picked up for her at the airport gift shop. I told her all about Hemmingway's house and the cats and coconut hulls. Finally she retreated to her room with her gifts, and I called the recorder.

I'd just finished patting the organic hamburger meat into burgers when I finally picked up conversation over my phone lying on the counter. I quickly washed my hands, turned the speakerphone off and held the phone to my ear. I only heard Baker's voice, so I assumed he was holding a phone to his ear, too.

"Joanna? I just got in about an hour ago," he said, followed by silence that seemed to last for eons.

"No, everything is okay, but I think you and the boys should stay in Gulfport for a few more days. Just stay there until everything blows over."

More silence. And more.

"I'll tell you everything when you get home…" He paused. "No, we don't have to worry about Leigh anymore."

My heart dropped.

TWENTY

When I woke Saturday morning, I immediately sprinted to the kitchen window to spy on Baker's home. Surprisingly, Joanna's car was parked in the driveway. She had ignored his advice to stay away for a few more days. She'd come home in the middle of the night to be with her murdering lover, and I was kicking myself for missing the juicy, informative conversation they must've had when she arrived.

Baker's car wasn't parked in its usual spot. His animal clinic was open until noon on Saturdays, so he must have been at work. It was time for this to end.

I fixed pancakes and sausage (gluten-free flapjacks and organic, humanely-raised pork) for my family while texting Rusty. He said he was slicking his hair back and would soon be over to present Joanna with a new vacuum attachment and retrieve the listening device from beneath Kilpatrick's kitchen table.

Tim and the girls joined me for breakfast, and then my husband left for a real estate showing. Soon my sleepy summer daughters had full bellies, and they camped out on the couch and watched television.

When I was done cleaning the kitchen, I told them I was going outside to work in the flower bed with Grace. I grabbed my phone and a cup of coffee, walked out the door and sat on the wrought iron bench nestled between the overgrown hydrangea and lavender crepe myrtle.

Rusty's mother's pewter van was soon pulling into Baker's driveway, and I called the recorder. Grace sat next to me on the bench, her visor nestled in her gray curls. She leaned over and pulled a blade of grass from the steaming mulch.

"You hear anything yet?" she asked.

I shook my head as Rusty walked to the front door in his church clothes with a duffel bag over his shoulder and some kind of vacuum brush dangling from his hand.

"I'll say it again. The boy looks good cleaned up. Not so Woodstock-y, you know? I was at Woodstock. I know what Woodstock-y looks like," she mumbled.

"*You* were at Woodstock, Grace?" I looked at her as the sound of the doorbell across the street chimed through my phone.

"Oh yes, dear!" She beamed with pride. "I was quite the rebel back in the day. Jack and I went when we were mere newlyweds. We did things that weekend that would…" She giggled and blushed. "Well, we had a good time."

I chuckled at her and looked back across the street. The navy blue door opened and Rusty walked into the home. Soon I heard his voice over the phone.

"I can't believe I forgot to give you this when you purchased the Rexair last week. Silly me!" Rusty laughed. "I came by yesterday but no one was home."

"Oh," Joanna replied. "Yeah, I had to go down to Gulfport for a few days while my fiancé was in Florida on business."

"She said Baker was in Florida on business," I repeated to Grace.

"Tsk. The killing business." Grace crossed her arms.

"Well, I'm glad I caught you. You'll be glad to have this attachment," Rusty said.

"What is it exactly?" Joanna asked with a hint of confusion in her tone.

"It's an upholstery tool. Deeply embedded dirt can drastically affect the life of fabric. This baby will have your upholstered furniture looking new," Rusty answered. "Would you like for me to demonstrate it for you?"

"He's going to demonstrate the upholstery tool," I informed Grace.

"The boy really should consider selling vacuums," Grace suggested. "It may be his calling."

The Rainbow roared to life and Rusty began loudly praising how it delicately sucked the dander from a throw pillow. I was snickering at his sales pitch until I saw the BMW turn onto our cove from Highway 78.

"Grace!" I exclaimed. "Baker is coming!"

"Oh, dear!"

"What do we do? Oh, mercy, what do we do, Grace?" I

panicked.

The sound of the vacuum continued to bellow through the phone as Baker parked his car next to the mini-van. He studied Mrs. Ballard's grocery getter for a second and then walked into his house.

"Oh heavens!" Grace leaned close to me. "What do you hear?"

I tightly gripped the phone between my right ear and her left. The vacuum soon shut off.

"What's going on?" Baker's voice came over the line.

"Hello, sir. I'm your local independent Rainbow Distributor, Russell." Rusty played the part well.

"I bought the Rexair from him last week," Joanna added.

"Do I know you?" Baker asked as I gripped Grace's arm with my free hand.

"I don't think so," Rusty said very casually.

"I do know you." Baker was adamant. "Wait. You were hanging around with the old lady next door. You were the one helping her steal cable, weren't you?"

"I knew I recognized you!" Joanna exclaimed. "You're that hippie but all cleaned up!"

"Sir. Ma'am," Rusty said, and then chuckled. "I don't steal cable. I sell high-quality vacuum cleaners."

"Yes, it was you. Russell? What's your last name?"

"Ballard," Rusty answered, and I would bet his face showcased that he immediately regretted divulging his real last name.

"Ballard? Ballard. How do I know that name?" Baker questioned. "Ralphie Ballard! He sells vacuums. You know him?"

"He's my brother, sir," Rusty reluctantly replied.

We suddenly heard a scuffle, possibly a chair sliding across the hardwood as Baker charged Rusty, followed by Joanna screeching Baker's name.

"What are you doing here?" Baker asked angrily through the sound of gritted teeth.

"I'm demonstrating an upholstery attachment for your fiancé, sir."

"Did Leigh send you?" Baker irately inquired.

"Leigh?" Joanna asked.

"Leigh?" Rusty repeated.

"Leigh?" Grace and I repeated Joanna and Rusty.

"Do you think Leigh is alive, Grace? Why would Baker ask Rusty that if she wasn't alive? She must be okay. He must've been lying to Joanna on the phone yesterday. He was just trying to pacify her when he told her they didn't have to worry about Leigh anymore! She must still be alive! He never found her!" I hoped aloud.

"I know your brother dated her!" Baker exclaimed. "I know you're the guy hanging around next door with the old lady. What are you doing here? What were you doing over there? Have you been spying on me? You been hanging around at the old lady's house so you could spy on me? Did Leigh send you? Tell me."

"Why have I always got to be referred to as an old lady?" Grace muttered.

"Leigh's dead, sir. How could a dead woman send me?" Rusty asked innocently.

"What do we do, Grace?" I interrupted the tense silence. "I feel helpless. I feel like Jimmy Stewart in *Rear Window*. Grace Kelly is in the house with Raymond Burr, and we're Jimmy Stewart sitting here helpless. What do we do? Call the police? Flash bulbs? Jimmy used flash bulbs. Do you have flash bulbs?"

"Quiet," she whispered.

"Really, sir, I honestly don't know what you mean. No one sent me. I'm not spying on you. I sell vacuums just like my brother does. I sold one to the old lady next door a few months back. While I was there, we started talking about cable. She asked if I could help her score that cat channel for free. Please don't report me, sir. I can't lose this job because I help the elderly steal cable on the side," Rusty said. "I didn't realize you were the guy Leigh left my brother for years ago until just now. Really, sir, I'm just a vacuum cleaner salesman."

"Get out of my house," Baker said sternly.

"Absolutely! I'll just get my bag and things off the kitchen table, and I'm out of here," Rusty agreed.

Static soon thundered over the line, and I placed the phone on my shivering, jumpy legs.

"You think he got it?" Grace asked. "He got the recorder?"

"I hope so." We both nervously watched the house.

Rusty bolted through the front door, and he discreetly flashed the small recorder concealed in the palm of his hand to us.

"Oh thank God!" I sighed and rubbed my face with my sweaty palms. "We should get inside before Baker sees the old lady spying on his house from my front yard."

I stood from the wrought iron bench. Rusty quickly reversed down the driveway and hauled the Caravan down the cove.

"That was exciting *and* scary." Grace slowly straightened her back and sipped her coffee. "Just like Woodstock."

TWENTY ONE

On Sunday morning, Tim and I sat on our usual pew (the fifth one from the front, on the right side) at Pontotoc Springs Baptist Church. Jules convened with her youth group at the very back where they wouldn't be seen giggling, passing notes and texting. Ellis was in children's church, thankfully still years away from being more occupied with text messaging than the Bible lesson. I talked quietly with my friend, Melinda, who always sat next to me. We were discussing Blair Merchant's unplanned seventh pregnancy when Chief Haskins plopped his hefty body on the empty oak pew in front of us and turned to face Tim.

"Chief," Tim said as he shook his pudgy hand and the pew creaked from the weight.

I tuned out Melinda's soft chatter and focused on their conversation. I noticed Grace observing them, as well, from her group of widowed blue-hairs on the left side of the sanctuary.

"Lavinia and I noticed the old house out on Chickasaw was for sale," he bellowed.

"Yes, sir, it is. Judge Talbot's old place went on the market last week," Tim confirmed.

"Well, Mary Kate recently got divorced, so she and the kids are moving back home with us. We'd like to just let her have the house. Lavinia and I were hoping to take a gander at Talbot's place. We've always loved that old farm." He used his sausage fingers to loosen the tight dress shirt choking his pink, tubby neck.

"I'd love to show it to you, Chief. Are you available this afternoon?"

"That sounds fine, Tim," he said as he pushed up from the pew. "I'll give you a call after lunch?"

"Yes sir. I'll run by the office on the way home and get the key."

"How are you, Tessa?" Chief then focused on me, sweat forming on his brow in the humid, old southern church.

"Just fine, Chief," I said, and then gulped.

"Obeying the speed limit I hope." He winked at me, referring to the frequent number of speeding citations I'd acquired over the years.

"Haven't had a ticket in three months and counting. They should give out milestone chips like in A.A.." I grinned.

"By golly!" He laughed heartily, and then it turned into a cough. "You've got a funny one there, Tim."

"Yes sir, I do," Tim said in agreement.

"See you later, son." He forcefully patted the shoulder of Tim's dress coat and wobbled down the aisle.

"Thanks, Chief," Tim called to him and then he leaned in to me. "Do you know the commission on that big old place? That sure would be nice."

"Sure would." Grace and I locked eyes and I shrugged at her.

How odd was it that Chief Haskins would talk to Tim that morning in church? We always spoke in passing, but rarely had a conversation with him. He and my husband would be together the very day that I would assemble a murder confession packet addressed to him. Talk about coincidence.

Or was it coincidence? Was this all part of an elaborate set up? Did Chief Haskins know I'd been conversing with my dead neighbor in Key West? Did he know that I'd been playing detective with an old lady and a hippie? Was he trying to get my husband out of the house and grill him for answers? My heart palpitated and now I was the one sweating in the humid, old southern church.

After service, we stopped by Tim's office for Talbot's key and ate a quick lunch at the Mexican place. I sprinted into the Dollar Tree next to the restaurant and purchased rubber dishwashing gloves and manila envelopes. As I was checking out, I realized that it was comparable to axe murderers shopping at Ace Hardware for duct tape and rope.

We arrived home, but Tim soon left to meet Chief Haskins. He took Ellis along. She was eager to tour the big, old mysterious farmhouse that sat at the end of Chickasaw Road. Jules' friend,

Samantha, had come home with us from church and they retired to Jules' room to undoubtedly gorge on stashes of candy and talk about boys.

I changed into running shorts and a tank top and walked over to Grace's house to prepare the package. Rusty met me there, this time driving his father's diesel truck. It roared into the privacy of Grace's garage so Baker wouldn't spot him going into the old lady's house.

"I burned the flash drive onto CD," Rusty said as he sat his messenger bag on Grace's dining table, next to her purring General and the stack of photos that I'd taken from her roof.

"What does that even mean?" Grace called from the kitchen where she was brewing a pot of coffee.

"I didn't want to be heard on the recording, so I had to edit out the conversation I had with Joanna while I was over there last time. On the CD, I copied only the murder confession and Baker's last phone conversation with Joanna after returning home from Key West. That's all the evidence Chief needs anyway. He doesn't have to hear them swapping spit while she defrosted herself a Kid Cuisine."

"Did you hear him tell her anything about Leigh? I mean, when she came home from Gulfport in the middle of the night? Did he say anything about his trip to Key West? Did he say anything about seeing me?" I questioned.

"No." Rusty shook his head. "They must've had that conversation somewhere else in the house."

I put on the thick latex gloves and took the CD from Rusty. I dusted it with a soft cloth to remove any fingerprints and stuck it inside the manila envelope.

"We should've covered the entire place with plastic. Like a kill room on *Dexter*," I worried aloud.

"No, I think we're okay." Rusty rolled his eyes at my precaution.

"I just don't want them to trace any of this back to us." I sighed. "Look! There's a cat hair stuck to that photograph! General could get pegged for this entire thing!"

"I don't think they're going to analyze a cat hair, Tessa."

"General! Get away from that mess!" Grace shuffled into the kitchen with her cup of coffee and shooed the orange cat from the dining table.

With salad tongs, I picked up the photos, dusted them with the cloth to remove the cat hair and any forensic evidence. I carefully slid them into the envelope, too.

"You cropped the photos so no one can tell they were taken from my roof?" Grace sat at the table.

"Yes. I zoomed in, reversed them and edited them so no one can even tell they are on Baker's back porch. All you can see is their faces pressed together. Those photos could've been taken at Trolley's Diner or the flea market. No one will know they were shot from your roof," I replied.

I'd removed all of the original tape from the post card because I was sure it had picked up one of my prints when I was piecing it together. I wore gloves to apply fresh tape, which deemed to be a real pain in the ass. Apparently tape likes to stick to rubber gloves.

Rusty handed me a letter that he had typed, explaining the entire situation and what could be heard on the CD, but careful not to give us away. I used the tongs to put it in the package, also.

Using awkward capital letters that looked nothing like my handwriting, I addressed the envelope to Haskins in bold, permanent marker. I wiped it down with the dusting cloth again, and again, and once more, as Rusty stood in the corner and appeared annoyed at my diligence.

"For Heaven's sake, Tessa, your prints aren't even in the system. Mine aren't. Grace's aren't. If they do find a print and run it, they won't even get a match. You're being a tad paranoid," he scoffed.

"Alright." I ignored him. "I think it's ready. Do you want to ride with me to the Itawamba Post Office, Rusty?"

"Why do we have to go all the way to Itawamba? I can mail it in Tupelo on my way home."

"No!" I demanded. "I want to mail it from some random, far-off place. The further it's sent from my house, the better."

"Well, let's just drive down to Pensacola and mail it. It'll only take, what, eight hours to get there? We can mail the letter, take a dip in the Gulf and come right back home. Really, Tessa, this is ridiculous."

"Look, I'm not taking any chances. You want to do time for posing as a vacuum salesman and planting a wire? If you'd rather write Cody's smoke story from prison and ask some burly con named Bubba to brainstorm synonyms for cough, well, that's fine with me. I have plenty of other things I can do on Tuesdays."

"Okay," he groaned reluctantly.

"Lovely." I smiled at him. "Now ride with this old lady to Itawamba."

I checked in with Jules and sent Tim a text to let him know I was going to run errands. I drove over to Grace's, and Rusty bolted to my SUV and slouched down in the seat so he wouldn't be seen with me as we passed Baker's home.

"Maybe I should stay away on Tuesdays for a while? I don't want him to see me anywhere near here," Rusty called from the floorboard of my Tahoe.

"That's probably a good idea," I agreed.

We drove east through Tupelo, and headed for the sticks of Itawamba County. We discussed the scandalous events of the summer, and Rusty chortled at the visual of me sliding off the roof in Jack's huge clothes with a spoon in my mouth. My phone interrupted his cackling, and I picked it up from the cup holder to see my mother's name.

I mumbled expletives under my breath.

"Who is it?"

"My mother," I said while pressing the red reject button.

"Tell me more about this beef with your mom. What'd she do so terrible that you refuse to answer her calls?"

"She abandoned my sister and me. She pawned us off on our grandparents because she didn't want us after our dad died." I kept my eyes on the steamy Mississippi two-lane.

"Maybe she was just doing what was best for you?" He

watched the green woods out the passenger side window. "Maybe she knew she wasn't emotionally capable to care for you after he died?"

"She could've made more of an effort with us, though. The nerve she had to show up at my wedding in that skanky outfit with that rebel on her arm! She only calls when she needs something from me. She doesn't even send my girls birthday cards or Christmas presents. She's been awful to us," I declared.

"Well," he said and shrugged, "she's still your mother."

"Why do people keep saying that?" I glanced at him. "You and the drunken lady in Florida both said that, as if I'm supposed to have a relationship with her just because we share blood. She may be my biological mother, but she's no real mother to me."

"Okay, okay," he said to pacify me.

"She's never apologized to me for anything. Maybe if she admitted how crappy she's been, we could start over. But she's too stubborn to ever acknowledge she's done me wrong."

"Maybe, but how could she ever apologize if you won't answer her calls?" he asked.

I laughed bitterly. "She won't apologize."

"She might," he said. "People change, Tessa."

"Not my mother." I turned into the gravel parking lot of the Itawamba Post Office.

I circled the Tahoe around the small, brick building and looked for security cameras. My heart began to palpitate and my palms became clammy.

"We should have rented a car," I worried out loud as I pulled next to the blue mailbox at the side of the post office. "A security camera is going to record my license plate, my gloved hand putting this package in this mailbox. It'll all be over then! I'll be called in for questioning, and I'll get diarrhea of the mouth, like always, and then I'll confess why I really went to Key West. I'll be charged as an accessory after the fact or something. They'll make a Lifetime movie about it, and I'll be the lead actress telling this story in an orange jump suit from a jail cell. We're going to get caught! They'll hire some grungy B-list actor to play you. Blythe Danner will portray Grace!"

Rusty sighed. "I really think we're okay. Just mail the stupid thing."

I pulled the yellow gloves from the console, and struggled to stretch them over my perspiring hands. I grabbed the heavy manila envelope from the back floorboard and wiped it down again with a dust rag. Rusty bit his tongue as I exhaled and then carefully stuck the package out of my rolled-down window and dropped it in the slot. It made a loud thump when it hit the bottom of the metal box. Then I removed the gloves and looked to him sitting in the passenger seat.

"Well, that's that." I raised my eyebrows. "So, have you thought of anymore synonyms for cough?"

TWENTY TWO

Five days had slowly passed since I'd mailed Baker's confession to Chief Haskins. I spent the time nervously gnawing on my fingernails and glancing out the window to his home across the street, anxiously awaiting squad cars and an armored van to roar onto his green Bermuda grass. A SWAT team would knock down the navy blue door with a battering ram and zip line into the upstairs window, glass shattering. They would drag Baker out of his home and throw him into the van. I waited for it, expecting it any second, but as of Friday afternoon, nothing had happened.

I clicked the ball point pen and stared at the first page of my manuscript, that first page that was stained with ink nearly six years old. I began scratching through all of words that referenced France, and replaced them with the port town in Southern Florida. The Monegasque thug, Pascal d'Aubigny, now hailed from Las Tunas and answered to Filiberto Rosada. Penelope kept her name, but her past was altered. She was no longer a French native working at a resort in Monte Carlo. Born and raised in Baton Rouge, she served as a poolside bartender at the Casa Marina in Key West. She spoke Louisiana Creole when she was scared or nervous.

For the first time in years, I was on a roll. I wrote fervently and passionately. I ignored the cramp in my hand as I scribbled vivid scenes of Penelope and Filiberto frolicking on the Florida beaches, drinking rum on Duval Street. When Penelope witnessed him execute a Cuban drug dealer, they fled down canal streets. He stripped the blood-splattered shirt from his back and tossed it into a dumpster as she panted, "Ce que vous pensiez, idiot!"

My arm ached from pressing the pen into the notebook paper. As the words flowed freely from my fingers, I lost all track of time. I was oblivious to Tim and the girls coming and going through the kitchen, popping tarts, fixing sandwiches, asking me questions, taking the dog out to pee. I was in the zone. Penelope, Filiberto and I were in our own world. We were in our own world– fleeing for our lives, hiding in an abandoned boat, contemplating confessions. For the first time in nearly six years, I was a writer with clear vision.

I could have sat at my kitchen island penning the story of Penelope Broussard for another three hours, five hours, all night. I could finish this book today, tomorrow, if I was allowed the time to focus solely on it. I could conquer this story, I could reach the climax, bring it back down, wrap it all up if I could block out all outside distractions. However, I couldn't ignore the sound of the doorbell.

I stood from the wrought-iron stool, my back aching from being slumped over the manuscript for so many hours. I straightened my spine and shuffled to the front door.

Through the peephole, I saw Chief Haskins standing with a young man at his side. My heart leapt into my chest, vomit threatened to escape my lips, and my knees buckled. I threw my back against the door and contemplated hiding beneath the foyer table until they went away. Or, better yet, flushing all the cocaine down the toilet and escaping through the bathroom window. There wasn't any cocaine in my home, and I suddenly realized I'd seen *Goodfellas* one too many times.

I took a deep breath then turned and wrapped my sweaty hand around the doorknob. I slowly opened the heavy door and produced an exact replica of my Starkville High 1994 Sweetheart Pageant smile. There was a lot of head tilting and teeth involved.

"Chief?" I squeaked.

"Hey there, Tessa." He appeared to be sweating bacon bits in the July humidity. "Mind if we come in?"

"Sure thing," I said while swallowing the lump in my throat and opening the door wider for them to enter the foyer.

"I know Tim's gone with Lavinia out to see the Chickasaw property again," he said.

He is? I thought. I was completely unaware of Tim telling me this detail. I didn't even know he'd left the house. I'd been so caught up in my book that I didn't even know what was going on in my own home. Where were my children? What day was it? When was the last time I peed? Because I suddenly needed to urinate now.

"She has really taken a liking to that old place. She's already picked out paint colors for the dining room and kitchen, but don't tell Tim that," he added, laughing. "We don't want him to know we're too eager to buy. Hoping he can convince the owners to knock a little more off the price first!"

"I understand that." I ushered them into the living room. "Can I get you anything? Water? Unsweetened tea?" *Handcuffs to slap on my wrists?*

"No thank you, Tessa. We'd just like to talk for a few minutes. Mind if we have a seat?" He nodded toward the couch.

"Sure," I replied and followed behind them, the loose collar of my t-shirt feeling more like a tight faux-turtleneck dickie strangling my neck. "Everything is okay I hope?"

"Oh yes." He plopped his huge body down onto the linen sofa, suffocating my favorite paisley throw pillow. "Well, mercy. I didn't even introduce you two. This is investigator Kyle Canady, Tessa. He's with the Tupelo Police Department."

"Hello," I said and smiled at the young kid who was probably still a speck in his father's eye while I was watching episodes of *LA Law* with Nanny.

"I wanted to ask you a few questions about your neighbor, Kilpatrick." Chief used his stubby hands to pull his leg the size of a tree trunk over his other leg.

"Oh?" I coughed as beads of sweat popped out of every pore on my face.

"What do you know about the fella?" he asked as the young detective caught my darting eyes and then wrote on a small notepad. I was certain he was noting, *Profuse perspiration. She's guilty of something.*

"Well, I've only talked to him a handful of times," I said and scratched my head.

The young detective wrote again. Probably, *She touched her head when she denied knowing the suspect. Nervous tick? She's guilty of something.*

"You haven't noticed anything suspicious at his home?" Chief inquired.

"No." I cleared my throat. "I don't think so. He seems to be a very private person. I rarely see him outside or anything."

"Did you know his wife? Mrs. Leigh Kilpatrick?" Kyle Canady asked.

"NO!" I said entirely too loud as the investigator wrote on his notepad again. "I met her when they moved in, but that was it. She seemed like a very private person as well."

"Can you tell me if you've seen any new vehicles or people at his home, Tessa? Have you seen anything different over there?"

"Well, yes," I said. "There's an older Honda over there a lot now. I've seen a redheaded girl and some young boys coming and going a few times. I assumed they were his kids or something. I don't know anything about the man really."

"You're aware Leigh Kilpatrick died though, correct?" Kyle questioned, the pen in his hand, eager to write adjectives such as, *nervous, sweaty, guilty.*

"Oh, yes," I said. "Grace McKinney and I saw her being wheeled out on a stretcher the morning she died. Dr. Parker told me she committed suicide. Tragic thing, isn't it?" I nervously crossed my arms and then quickly un-crossed them.

I heard the sound of Jules' socked feet and Oreo's toenails shuffling across the hardwood flood.

"Hello, dear." Chief looked past me to Jules entering the living room.

"Hi." She smiled and took a seat next to me. "Mama, what's going on?"

"They're asking some questions about Mr. Kilpatrick." I tucked her long hair behind her ear.

"So you've never talked to him, Tessa?"

"Not really, no." I shook my head adamantly.

"He saved my dog," Jules chimed in as I tensely chewed on the inside of my cheek.

"He did?" The young investigator spoke.

"You didn't tell him he saved Oreo?" Jules asked me as the

dog jumped into her lap.

"Oh, my." I nervously chuckled. "I'd forgotten all about that."

"What happened with the dog?" Chief asked Jules.

"He got bit by a snake in the backyard. Mr. Kilpatrick rushed him to his clinic and saved him. He didn't have to do that. He wasn't even working that day." Jules rubbed Oreo's dark ears.

"Well that was awful kind of him, wasn't it?" Chief Haskins shrugged.

"Yes, he's a great veterinarian," I mumbled. "Other than that, though, I don't know anything about him. That was the first time I've ever really spoken to him."

"How long ago did this episode happen with the dog?" Kyle asked.

"Um…I don't know," Jules said and glanced at me. "A few weeks ago I guess."

"He didn't say anything about his wife or the redhead while he was caring for your dog on his day off?"

"No sir, not a word. We talked about the dog and that was it. I don't know anything about his wife's murder." I immediately closed my eyes and prayed I hadn't really said murder.

"Murder? Who said his wife was murdered?" Kyle leaned forward on the couch.

"Did I say murder?" I chuckled. "Oh good heavens, I meant suicide, of course."

"But you said murder," Kyle pressed me.

"She's writing a murder mystery," Jules answered. "She's always got murder on the brain."

I smiled widely and nodded enthusiastically; thankful my daughter was there to save me. "I was just working on the book when you rang the doorbell. I've been writing non-stop for hours. I do have murder on the brain."

"Murder mystery, eh?" Chief chuckled. "Those are Lavinia's favorite. You'll autograph a copy for her I hope?"

"Absolutely!" I exclaimed.

Still, the young detective didn't look convinced at the reason for my slip up. He eyed me for a few seconds and went back to his notepad.

"Well, Tessa," Chief groaned as he prepared to heave his body from the low sofa, "I think that's all we need."

"Can I ask what this is all about? Has Baker done something?" I stood from the corduroy chair.

"We aren't sure yet. We've just had some things come to our attention. I'm sure it's nothing." Chief gripped the arm of the couch and pulled himself to his large feet. "I can trust you won't mention our visit?"

"My lips are sealed." I pretended to zip my mouth shut. "Let me know if I can do anything to help."

"You can help by coming forward if you see anything strange over there." Kyle Canady's eyes locked with mine. He was suspicious of me, I just knew it.

"And what exactly would be considered strange, Mr. Canady?"

"Well, Mrs. Lambert, you're the murder/mystery writer. I'm sure you'll be able to recognize anything peculiar," he retorted.

"We've taken enough of your time, Tessa." Chief Haskins lead Kyle out the front door. "We're going to pay Mrs. Grace a visit now. Have a good afternoon."

"Thanks," I said.

"And don't tell Tim what I said about Lavinia loving the house too much, you hear?" He pulled a handkerchief from his pocket and wiped his shiny, sweaty forehead.

"Yes sir." I grinned and shut the door before pressing my back to it again and sliding to the floor.

"Mama?" Jules looked at me oddly from the living room. "Are you okay?"

"Yeah," I said. "I just get nervous around the Fuzz."

"Anyone who still calls the police "the Fuzz" probably has nothing to be nervous about." She and Oreo left me alone to exhale for ten full seconds and wipe the sweat from my brow.

TWENTY THREE

On Sunday morning, as I quickly ironed Ellis' church clothes while scanning the bathroom vanity for my favorite earrings, the phone rang. I lifted the steaming iron from the pastel maxi dress and looked over to see my mother's name flashing on the caller ID. I sighed, but hesitated before ignoring the call.

"Tim, I need to answer this. Will you finish ironing Ellis' dress for me? It's Karen."

"Sure." He stepped out of his closet in his boxer shorts and t-shirt. "Don't let her put you in a funk before church."

"Hello?" I answered and walked down the hallway towards the kitchen.

"Tessa?" she responded in her deep voice.

"We're trying to get ready for church. What do you need?" I was impatient with her. I didn't want to be late for church because she needed to borrow a few hundred dollars for new chaps to wear on the ride to Sturgis.

"I just wanted to talk to you for a few minutes. Should I call back later?" she sincerely offered.

"No, it's fine," I stuttered, stunned at her suggestion to call back when it was more convenient for me. "What do you need?"

"I don't need anything, really. I just wanted to talk to you. But if I should call back—"

"No, it's okay," I replied, confused. "Talk."

"I've, um, well, I've been doing some thinking," she stammered.

I silently looked out the window to Baker's home.

"I've been, well, I've been thinking about why my daughters won't answer my calls or, you know, why you always sound so disgusted to talk to me," she paused and then cleared her throat. "For a long time, I didn't, well...I didn't see my part in that. I just thought, I really thought, I just had ungrateful daughters."

"Ungrateful?" I began.

"But I realize there's nothing for you to be grateful for, Tessa."

She sounded ashamed. My mother, who let her breasts nearly fall onto my wedding alter, sounded ashamed. "I, um, I've been talking with a counselor for a few weeks, and well, I know I need to own up to my mistakes."

My mouth dropped open in shock. Was this my mother on the other end of the line? I double checked the number on the phone. It had to be her. No one else possessed such a deep drawl, except maybe Darth Vader with laryngitis.

"I'm…" She hesitated, "I'm sorry I pawned you and Darcy off on your grandparents when you were young, Tessa."

I didn't know how to respond. I just stood there at the kitchen window in my slip and hot rollers, stunned by the words coming from my mother's lips.

"Your father was the love of my life. When he died, such a large part of me died with him, and I couldn't, well, to be honest, I couldn't be around you and Darcy after he was gone. It was, um, too painful for me, as crazy as that sounds."

"What do you mean?" I quickly wiped my teary eyes with the back of my hand.

"You both remind me so much of him. Your eyes and nose, your mannerisms. You, especially, are Kent Ellis made over. You were the spitting image of him when you were only three, and you still are. It was hard for me to look at you day in and day out and constantly be reminded that he was never coming back."

"Why are you saying all of this now?" I began nervously gnawing on my peach fingernail.

"I've just been so, I've been, so unhappy for a long time now. Through some mutual friends, I was introduced to this counselor who works at the big Baptist church down on Hawkins, and I decided to pay her a visit. She's been helping me work through a lot of issues for a few weeks now. She put a big mirror in front of my face, and I don't like what I see," my mother said as I squeezed my eyes shut to contain the tears. "I know I can't make over 30 years of mistakes right with one phone call, but I just want to, well, Tessa, I want to apologize for a lot of things. Maybe I could do that in person? Maybe I can come spend a few days with you and Darcy? I think we have a lot to talk about."

"Yeah." I sniffled. "That would be really good."

"You'll check your schedule and get back with me then? Talk to Darcy for me? She won't answer my calls. Maybe you could convince her to meet with me while I'm there?"

"Yeah," I said. "I can do that. We'll work something out."

"I won't bring any bikers with me. I'll, um, I'll come alone. No bikers named after insects. No smoking, either." I could picture her smiling.

"Alright." I grinned. "That sounds great."

"Okay, Tessa. Go get ready for church. We'll talk soon?"

"Sure," I said, prepared to hang up. "Bye."

"Oh, Tessa," she interrupted me. "How are Tim and the girls?"

I smiled as a tear raced down my cheek. "They are fine. They're fine, Mom."

"I look forward to catching up with them, too."

"Thanks for calling."

"Bye, Tessa."

"Bye." I pulled the phone from my ear to hang it up, but I swore I heard my mother say, "I love you."

As I tried to process the phone call with my mother, with my "new and improved" mother who seemed to, for the first time, possess a guilty conscious, a moral compass, compassion, empathy and remorse, my thoughts were interrupted by the sight of police cars pulling up Baker Kilpatrick's steep driveway.

"It's happening. It's really happening," I whispered. "Tim! Come here!"

He soon entered the kitchen in his khaki pants and unbuttoned dress shirt with his blue tie hanging from his hand.

"What did your mother have to say?" he asked.

"Not now. Look at this."

He came closer and stood next to me at the kitchen window.

"What's going on? This is about them interviewing you Friday?" he asked as we watched Chief Haskins, Kyle Canady and several uniformed officers climb the steps onto Baker's front porch.

"I guess so." I shrugged. "I told you he's done something terrible!"

The navy blue door opened and Baker stepped onto the porch, closing it behind him. Chief Haskins began speaking to him.

"Overactive imagination, my foot! That man is guilty of terrible things. I've known it since day one," I stated.

"We don't know why they are there, Tessa. This doesn't mean he's in trouble. We don't know..." His voice trailed off.

We continued to observe the meeting on Baker's front porch. He slowly turned around and one of the uniformed officers placed handcuffs on his wrists.

"Oh, we don't, eh?" I punched my husband in the arm. "I told you, Tim! I told you!"

Tim watched in disbelief as Baker was escorted down his front porch steps, barefoot, in pajama pants and a t-shirt. His dark hair was disheveled, his face covered in day-old stubble. He kept his eyes low, staring at the pavement beneath his bare feet, and they placed him in the back of a squad car. He looked guilty. Baker Kilpatrick looked guilty of killing his sister-in-law, staging his wife's death, having her murdered 90 miles from Cuba. It was natural to see him in the back of that police car. He looked at home. That's where he had belonged for weeks, maybe years, because God only knew what he'd done in his past.

Joanna then appeared in the doorway and talked with Chief Haskins and the officers for a few minutes. She disappeared into the house and then walked back out with the two young boys. They marched down the porch steps and climbed into the back of Chief Haskins' Impala.

"That's his lover. He killed for her," I told Tim.

"You don't know that," Tim mumbled quietly, intently studying the scene across the street.

"Oh, but I do know that." I chewed my nails. "Grace! I've got to call her!"

The phone was still in my hand from the conversation with my mother, and I frantically dialed Grace's landline.

"Hello?" she asked.

"Are you watching this?" I barked. "Tell me you're watching this!"

"Watching what? I'm ironing my slacks for church," she replied.

"Forget the slacks! Get to your front window now. It's going down, Gray Goose. It's going down!" I was so excited that I nearly jumped up and down.

I could hear Grace shuffling to the front of her house, her phone rustling against her ear.

"What did you call her? Gray Goose?" Tim questioned.

I placed my hand over the phone and told him, "That's her secret agent name."

"Well, my word! What's going on? They finally got him, did they?" Grace shouted.

"They just put him in the back of a car," I said. "The redhead and the boys are in the Impala."

"I didn't tell them anything to give us away on Friday," Grace assured me. "They don't think I know anything."

"I'm just glad to see he finally got what he deserved. We knew it the whole time, didn't we, Grace?"

We silently held the phone to our ears as the cars containing Baker, Joanna and the twins reversed down the driveway. They slowly moved down the street and then took a right on Highway 78 towards Tupelo.

"Well," Tim said. "That's interesting."

The young investigator, Kyle, and two officers stayed behind. They entered Baker's home and shut the navy blue door behind them.

"Must be looking for evidence." Tim turned away from the window and buttoned his shirt. "Evidence for what, I don't know."

"Evidence that he killed his wife, of course, Tim."

"Well, dear," he answered, pulling the tie through the collar of his shirt as he left the kitchen, "you may have been right all along."

I grinned like a Cheshire cat and called out to him, "Of course I was! Why did you ever doubt me, dear?"

"You think she made it out of Key West alive?" Grace spoke into the phone. "Leigh? You think she's okay?"

"I don't know, but I sure do hope so."

"Well, we may never know, but that's that." Grace sighed into the phone. "You did good, Cagney."

"So did you, Lacey. So did you."

LEIGH

I stepped off the plane, overjoyed to be engulfed by the frosty October air. Beaming from ear to ear, I retrieved my luggage and immediately began my search for a hat shop. I bounded into the first one I saw and purchased a grey rabbit fur ushanka. It's so beautiful and plush and does a marvelous job at helping to keep me warm here in Yakutsk.

I almost didn't make it to this beautifully frigid place. Baker almost won. He almost caught me. He almost did exactly what Tessa Lambert had warned me he would do.

I saw him the day after I met with Tessa at Sloppy Joe's Bar on Duval Street. I'd spent the morning hiding in my apartment, contemplating what to do with my former neighbor's information. When I stepped out for the first time early that afternoon to grab a bite to eat, my handsome Baker was standing on the corner of Caroline and Margaret, showing a group of pedestrians what I assumed was my photo. My heart nearly exploded in my chest as I sprinted behind a palm tree and a row of penny saver stands.

While he was occupied with the people on the corner, I ducked into Hammerhead's. An acquaintance, Sylvia, was working. I explained that my husband had come looking for me. I told her he was abusive and may have meant to cause me harm, and then I pleaded for her help. Being a former battered woman, Sylvia was eager to aid me in escaping Baker's malicious plot.

She let me hide in the stock room of the surf shop while her younger brother manned the register. Still, I could see out the small side window to the corner where Baker was conversing with passersby, flashing them my picture, his dark hair tousled by the salty wind. I watched Sylvia approach him and begin speaking.

She told him that she knew the girl in the photo, and that I'd left for Mississippi a few days ago; that I'd told everyone I was going back home to my husband. Baker believed her, bless his heart, and the panic on his face proved it. He hadn't traveled this far south to reunite with me, take me into his arms or to start a new life with me as we had originally planned. Baker had come to Key West to tell me goodbye, to quite possibly have me executed as Tessa had predicted.

When they were through talking, Baker turned and nearly raced down the street. I assumed he was eager to catch the first flight back home. He was anxious to stop me before I showed up at our navy blue door on Sugar Creek Cove.

I wept for ten solid minutes in that surf shop stock room. I wept for my failed marriage, for my sister's murder, for my naiveté and mistakes and the years of drug abuse. I wept and Sylvia let me, uninterrupted, onto a box of tank tops and shark-tooth key chains.

I didn't know if Baker had seen Tessa while he was in Key West, but I certainly hoped he hadn't. Despite the feelings of envy and disgust that I'd always possessed for that perfect blonde suburbanite, she'd saved my life. She'd risked her own to warn me. In an alternate universe, I would quite possibly call Tessa Lambert my friend.

Drying my eyes, I thanked Sylvia and headed to my rented duplex on Margaret Street. I gathered all of my belongings, including the cash that I'd brought with me to Key West. There was only $2,200 left. Knowing this wouldn't be enough to travel to the other side of the world, I began formulating plans to raise money— decent, legal plans.

I caught the 6:20 bus to Miami and checked into a cheap motel near the airport. That's where I stayed for nearly three months and studied the Russian rules of pronunciation. That's where I stayed while a guy in Little Havana perfected my new fake ID and passport. That's where I stayed while I saved the money I earned waitressing at Rolando's Diner— while I saved the money that would start my new life in an ushanka hat.

This is where I was meant to be. No heat or humidity. Snow, beautiful snow, covers the sidewalks and the Lada's hoods as they sail down white streets. I've yet to trip over a cat or hear a Jimmy Buffett song.

The name on my fake ID reads Jody Pratt. I'm working as an

English translator at Yakutia Airlines and making decent money. I'm renting an apartment near the city centre. I'm lengthening my vowels, and I'm learning to understand consonant clusters. I've had some help from a handsome, broad-shouldered tutor named Alexey Stepanov. He's patient and gentle and wants to take Jody out for pelmeni. He would never hit me over the head with a Doc Marten or leave me in the heat to be annoyed by felines. He'd never stage my suicide, throw me over for a red-headed child or plot to have me murdered.

I sent a post card from Lena Pillars National Park a few days ago.

Tessa Lambert
430 Sugar Creek Cove
Pontotoc Springs, Mississippi 38288

Learning to make Kiev cake so I don't have to send you store-bought.

Thanks for everything.

I didn't sign my name, but I think she'll know it's from me.

.

TWENTY FIVE

While sitting at the kitchen island, I ran my hand across the stack of printed pages. Over the course of three months, *Penelope's Predicament* (working title) had been rewritten, rearranged, edited and reedited by Gabriella in New York. When I finally felt it was satisfactory to type into a Word document, I printed it, along with a query letter and full synopsis. It was finally ready to be sent to Gabriella's contacts in the publishing industry.

Five years of my life led up to this very moment. Five years of inaccurately envisioning the French Riviera, drinking gallons of Folgers, slamming pens down in frustration had led up to this very moment. Five years of mind constipation, anxiety, longing and desire had finally, thankfully, come to an end. Thank goodness Leigh Kilpatrick staged her suicide. If not, I'd never have a reason to travel to the southernmost point in the continental United States and be refreshed by Hemmingway.

I grabbed the sage wool cardigan draped over the kitchen chair and put it on. Picking up the heavy manuscript from the counter, I placed it in a manila folder addressed to New York, and then opened the kitchen door and stepped into the crisp autumn air.

Mr. Anderson has been burning oak leaves for two days. Ash rained down on my head and singed the back of my throat. He noticed me walking the driveway and lifted his arm. I returned the wave before he went back to monitoring the flaming burn pile and sang out a chorus of Elvis' "Burning Love".

I pulled the cardigan close to my body and eyed the For Sale sign stuck in Dr. Parker's manicured front lawn. His wife had recently accepted an ecologist position at the University of Southern Mississippi in Hattiesburg. His children weren't too happy about the move, but I was sure they'd soon find new pot dealers and adjust quite well. Before reaching the mailbox, I looked to the foreclosure sign placed in the Kilpatrick yard draped with leaves.

I opened the cold metal box and retrieved yesterday's stack of mail before placing the novel inside. I heaved a collective sigh of relief and shut the mailbox. Now I just needed a multi-million dollar book deal to bring this thing full circle.

"Finally sending it off?" Grace called from her front porch, her robe wrapped tightly around her body, steam rising from the cup of brew in her hand.

"Yes ma'am." I gave her a thumbs up.

"I'm so proud of you, love. It's going to be a best seller," she shouted. "I knew you could do it."

"Thank you, Grace," I called back to her, my eyes welling up with tears at her compassionate and encouraging words.

Grace disappeared behind her front door, and I began walking up the driveway while flipping through the mail. When I saw a postcard of snowy, rocky formations along a river, labeled Lena Pillars National Park, I came to a stop. I flipped the card over and read the words. Then I read them again. And then I clutched the postcard to my chest and smiled.

When back in my warm kitchen and shielded from the ash and the cold, I studied the post card again. I wouldn't tell a soul that I'd received it. Not Grace or Rusty. Leigh Kilpatrick's Russian address was safe with me.

I thumbed through several bills and some junk mail. At the bottom of the pile was a white envelope with a Miami return address.

Dearest Tessa,

I so enjoyed getting to know you in Key West back in July. You were so refreshing (unlike those sticks in the mud from Minnesota). I hope Pete's plaid on plaid ensemble didn't take away from the other beauty that the Keys had to offer while you were there.

I'm eager to know if you've completed your novel. How did Key West work as the setting? I certainly can't wait to read it. Perhaps you could send me a signed copy when it's completed? I would cherish it always!

Since meeting you, you've inspired me to do a little writing, too. I've been working on a book of poetry about our home away from home. It's going quite well, and I find the creativity absolutely cathartic. I just wish I could find something to rhyme with "coconut".

Tessa, your relationship with your mother has also weighed heavily on my heart and mind. I do hope you've made amends with her. As you already know, I wish I had taken the chance to make things right with my mother when it was presented to me. I do hope that you're given that chance and you take full advantage of it. Life is too short to carry grudges and bicker. I hope you and your mother will both see that.

I felt that we had such a powerful connection. Perhaps we crossed paths for a reason? Maybe that I would influence you to forgive your mother? That you would help this old woman find passion in something other than drinking Key Lime martinis by the trough? Do let me hear from you, Tessa.

With love,

Verna

I would reply to Verna's letter and tell her that, yes, my mother and I were in a good place. She'd come up to visit for a few days in August. She looked good. She slapped a nicotine patch on her arm and wore shirts with collars that didn't draw attention to her tattooed cleavage.

We went back-to-school shopping for the girls. Darcy joined us, as well, and we had a lovely afternoon. At the food court in the mall, our mother bore her soul and shed tears over a plastic bowl of sweet and sour chicken. She took both my sister and me by the hand and asked us to forgive her for thirty-five years of selfishness. We did.

Mother regularly calls every week. She forwards me chain-letter emails and outlandish stories that have been verified as false by Snopes— just like my friends' mothers do. She texts me recipes and sends the girls "just because" gifts. She gave Tim her Van Morrison collection. She's making an effort, and I thank God for it.

I put both Verna's letter and Leigh's postcard in the pocket of the sage cardigan only moments before Rusty walked through my kitchen door on that Tuesday morning. His ratty messenger bag looked lighter without the typed copy of *Ten Speeds of Love* in it. He'd finished the story only a few days before and sent it to New York to be edited by a fellow young hippie. As a favor to me, Gabriella introduced the two.

"You really think Cody quitting cold turkey in the third chapter was a good idea?" He threw the man purse to the kitchen table and dusted ash from the sleeve of his oversized hoodie donning Bob Dylan's profile.

"Absolutely it was," I confirmed. "We didn't have to use words like lung butter even once! He was a strapping, healthy man and won the marathon, didn't he? He rode into the sunset with Mary sitting on his handlebars, didn't he? Quitting smoking was the best decision of his life."

"I know." He shrugged. "But smoking defined him."

"People change, Russell. Our quirks and hobbies and overactive imaginations don't define us." I stood to fix us both a cup of coffee.

Handing him a warm mug, we sat together at the farm table. We eyed the magnolia leaves swaying in the cool wind and the soot from Mr. Anderson's yard floating across the gray sky. I noticed we were both lightly tapping our fingers on the table. We were bored.

"So," I broke the silence. "Have you been following the trial?"

"Yeah, it isn't looking good for him, is it?" He nodded toward the empty house across the street. "I heard they matched the handwriting on the suicide note to the post card from Key West. They know for sure that Leigh didn't commit suicide in the house that day. They may exhume Laurel's body."

"I think he'll be put away for quite a while. Looks like Joanna may be in some trouble, too. She knew he was going to Key West with the intent to murder Leigh. She'll do some time for that I bet."

"You think she got away? Leigh? You think she made it out of Key West alive?" He sipped from the polka dot cup.

I secretly patted the post card in my pullover pocket. "I think she's doing just fine."

"Well?" He sighed. "What should we do now? You're finished with your book. I'm finished with mine. Penelope and Cody are out of our hands now."

I shrugged and looked back out the window.

"So we're done? You and me?" he asked with a hint of disappointment in his tone.

"Why, Rusty." I nudged him. "Are you implying that you enjoy working with me? You enjoy Tuesdays with Tessa?"

"No," he scoffed. "I don't know."

"Silly boy, you enjoy spending time with this old lady, don't you?" I laughed.

"Hey!" Rusty looked to me, wide-eyed, an idea brewing beneath that shaggy hair. "I know exactly what we can work on now!"

"What?" I sat the coffee cup to the table as he shot his eyes to the house with the foreclosure sign on the unkempt lawn.

"Rusty, no," I said. "We can't write about that."

"We'll change it up! Oh, Tessa! It's great material! We lived it, we can tell it. We'll just change the character's names and a few other details. We'll make it fiction!" He exclaimed before I argued with him.

"We'll make it fiction, Tessa! We'll even write you and Grace as *young* ladies! I'll be the top Rainbow salesman in the country! The troubled heroine will be on horse tranquilizers!" He pulled his laptop from his ratty messenger bag.

"No, Rusty," I said and stood from the table. I walked over to the catch-all drawer and retrieved my trusty ballpoint pen and a stack of notebook paper. "I don't type. I write."

Rusty beamed as I scribbled the following words at the top of the page:

Suspicion on Sugar Creek
Rusty Ballard and Tessa Lambert

ACKNOWLEDGMENTS

Like rap artists and movie stars, I first and foremost have to thank God. Seriously, though. I have to thank Him for placing within me the desire to pen poems about dogs and recess when I was just a little girl. I have to thank Him for giving me this beautiful outlet which I have finally learned to never take for granted. I have to thank Him for putting words and stories in my head and allowing me to call it "fiction" instead of "lies". Thank you, Lord, for every blessing You've given me. I'm so utterly unworthy of Your unfailing love, mercy and grace.

I started this novel a few months before my precious mother passed away on September 20, 2015. My mama loved humor and Hemmingway and Hitchcock. When I told her the premise for this book and that it would reference all three, she was ecstatic and couldn't wait to read it.

My mama instilled within me a love of God, a love of writing and a love of music– three of the most important things in my life. She was my biggest fan, my rock, my unwavering support, my sidekick. She was the funniest and most talented woman that I've ever had the beautiful pleasure of knowing this side of Heaven. She was this little girl's everything and the void without her by my side and in my life is indescribable.

It was an incredibly bittersweet moment to type the last line of this story. This is the first book I've completed since she's been gone. This is the first of my work that she'll never read or keep a copy of on her nightstand. I won't lie. That hurts.

So I acknowledge my mother here. I recognize her and thank her for raising me on her stories– factual stories of her youth, fictional stories about fairies and farms and characters with funny names. She encouraged me when I started writing at age 9, when God placed that desire within me, and she never stopped. She, too, was so talented with words– writing short stories, poems and songs on the piano, and there's never a time when I pick up a pen or type on a computer or play a piano that I don't think of her.

Thank you, Mama, for giving me life and making it good. I cannot wait to see you and Daddy hand in hand on the other side.

To my sweet children, Natalie Ann and Bennett Brown, thank you for contently eating pizza rolls when mama was too busy writing to make you a nutritionally balanced meal.

Thanks also to my editor, Jennifer Oradat, for your awesome suggestions and making sure grammatical errors and typos were at an all-time low. I appreciate all of your hard work.

To my multi-talented friend, Anna Lind Thomas, thank you for creating the cover of this book. I'm so glad that the good Lord brought us together. Although we are so far apart, I consider you one of my finest (and most hilarious) friends.

And last, but most absolutely, definitely and certainly not least, I have to extend gratitude to all of the blog followers, Facebook fans, friends, neighbors, local businesses, community centers, book clubs and perfect strangers who seem to delight in and happily share what I do. Your kindness and encouragement have helped make this southern girl's writing dreams come true. May God richly bless each and every one of you.

Hugs, kisses and all that jazz.
SBL